A TASTY TERROR . . .

"If one really wanted to introduce the juice from some poisonous plant into somebody's food or drink so that they didn't notice it, is there any such plant that doesn't have too strong a taste?"

"This really is going too far!" exclaimed Rosalind to her son.

Bernard seemed unperturbed by the question. "I would say that hemlock water dropwort is just such a plant. The yellow juice that comes from the stem and the root is a virulent poison, even more potent than the juice of the hemlock proper and with, so far as I know, no antidote. Apparently the taste is sweetish and by no means unpleasant. . . ."

"She never puts a foot wrong."
—H.R.F. Keating, *The Times*

Books by Anna Clarke
From The Berkley Publishing Group

POISON PARSLEY
ANNA CLARKE

BERKLEY BOOKS, NEW YORK

POISON PARSLEY

A Berkley Book / published by arrangement with
the author

PRINTING HISTORY
William Collins Sons & Co. Ltd. edition published 1979
Berkley edition / February 1992

ISBN: 0-425-13182-3

A BERKLEY BOOK ® TM 757,375
Berkley Books are published by The Berkley Publishing Group,
200 Madison Avenue, New York, New York 10016.
The name "BERKLEY" and the "B" logo
are trademarks belonging to Berkley Publishing Corporation.

PRINTED IN THE UNITED STATES OF AMERICA

10 9 8 7 6 5 4 3 2 1

"My heart aches, and a drowsy numbness pains
My sense, as though of hemlock I had drunk."

Ode to a Nightingale
—John Keats

POISON PARSLEY

—— 1 ——

They looked more like brother and sister than mother and son. Most people meeting Rosalind and Martin Bannister for the first time had this impression. She looked astonishingly young for a woman who had suffered for years from a violent drunkard of a husband and only narrowly escaped being convicted of his manslaughter, while Martin, only child of that unhappy marriage, looked old beyond his eighteen years.

When you got to know them a little better, though, you realized that in spite of the fact that they seemed to be such good friends, each had a deeply protective attitude towards the other very different from the more casual fraternal relationship. That was the general opinion of the village of Swallowfields in Sussex where they had made their home. There had been some initial doubt and suspicion, of course, because Rosalind had not attempted to deny that she was the Mrs. Bannister of the notorious "hammered husband" case. After all, she had killed John Bannister, one-time best-selling novelist but at the time of his death a bankrupt alcoholic, by throwing that hammer. It had, however, been proved to be an accident, without any intent to kill or even injure, and the details of the husband's behaviour, avidly read in the newspapers by the inhabitants of Swallowfields as well as the rest of the country, were such that one could only wonder why nobody had taken a hammer or a knife to him before.

On further acquaintance, Rosalind Bannister turned out to be one of those kind and gentle women who was fated to be exploited in one way or another. If she was not careful, she would end up by marrying just another such brute of a husband. She was attractive in a quiet and unassuming way, and neatly dressed; practical and efficient about the house, helpful to people in trouble, and an excellent listener. There was the son, of course, but he would be going away to university before long and would in due course become independent and no bar to his mother's remarriage.

Unfortunately for those who would have liked Rosalind Bannister to find a good husband, as well as for those who liked to prophesy that she would find another bad one, there were virtually no candidates for either office in the village of Swallowfields. Its period cottages and pleasant modern bungalows housed mostly elderly widows or middle-aged couples, the husbands commuting either to London or to one of the little pockets of industry tucked away in the landscape under the South Downs. Unattached ladies there were in plenty, but unattached men tended to flit away. There was the vicar, of course, but he was not the marrying kind, to put it tactfully. Besides, Rosalind Bannister never went to church.

She came to flower-arranging classes, however, and to other Women's Institute meetings that took place in the village community centre, and it was at one of these that she first met Bernard Goodwin, author and broadcaster on topics of the countryside and a newly-arrived resident of Swallowfields.

Bernard Goodwin was a delightful man, good-looking, friendly, knowledgeable but not so clever that he made you feel stupid and inferior. He was in his late fifties—just the right age for Rosalind—and obviously had plenty of money because he had bought Bell House, a substantial house a mile or two out of the village, with a large garden and plenty of outhouses where he could carry out his experiments with plants. Unfortunately he already had a wife, who had scarcely been seen in the village and who never turned up when he gave a talk to the Women's Institute on the medicinal uses of common plants. He was writing a book about the wonderful natural cures to be found growing in gardens and hedgerows, and the whole audience had caught his enthusiasm on the occasion of that meeting, to such a degree that women who lived alone began dosing themselves with garlic, and some of those with husbands began dousing themselves with rosewater, while others took the whisky glasses out of the hands of their weary spouses when they got back from work in the evening, and forced them to drink concoctions of camomile or cowslip instead.

Rosalind was not one of the most fanatical followers of Bernard Goodwin's suggestions, but she did have a short conversation with him after his lecture, which resulted in her brewing up some lemon balm into a drink that she persuaded Martin to take.

"Martin said I was balmy," she said laughingly to Lesley Green, a retired schoolteacher who shared Rosalind's interest in music and painting and was the nearest thing she had made to a friend in the village. "But I'm sure it's helped him through his A levels. He's not been nearly as edgy as he was and I'm going to tell Mr. Goodwin so if I see him again."

She did in fact see Bernard Goodwin again, not in the village hall this time in the presence of thirty other people, but alone on the footpath that led off the High Street a short distance from Rosalind's cottage and through the fields to the neighbouring village of Leahurst.

It was one of those softly glowing mornings in June that are almost too beautiful for the human senses to bear, and Rosalind was walking slowly alongside an overflowing hedgerow, her eyes on the lush grass and the wayside flowers, almost dreading to look up at the pleasant English countryside for fear of what the glory of the morning might do to her deadened heart. For this woman who had won herself toleration and a small place in a human community had done so only by exercising great patience and self-control, by deliberately creating a character that could offend nobody. Even with her son she had become something of a fake, and the fake was so successful that she managed to convince herself for much of the time that her own nature had changed completely and that she really had turned into this dim placid creature with no passion left in her.

Since Rosalind's new life had begun no human being had come anywhere near to exposing the fake. The threat to her defences came from other sources. Sitting alone in the living-room in her cottage, while Martin on the floor above struggled with his physics and maths, Rosalind sometimes felt a painful little stab, unconnected with any physical disorder or discomfort, at the sound of a Schubert quintet or an aria from a Mozart opera. The same sensation attacked her when she climbed the steep chalky path to the top of the Downs and saw the patchwork landscape emerge from morning mist beneath, or when she stood at the back door of the cottage in the evening and watched the last of the light in the sky fade between the two tall beech trees in the churchyard.

Music and natural beauty brought to Rosalind Bannister these first faint stirrings of sensation, as if she were coming round from an anaesthetic, and as the months passed they became more frequent and more intense, and she became more and more frightened of them. She was going for a long walk by herself on this fine June morning in order to take stock of the eighteen months she and Martin had lived in Swallowfields and to try to decide whether it was time to move on, but so far her thoughts had not been very constructive. All that happened was that the ache of loneliness swelled to an almost intolerable pain, and the only way to endure this bright day seemed to be to turn back and shut herself up in the scullery, which she used as a studio, and get down to painting some more of the table-mats that always sold best of all the little pieces of craftwork that she did. Perhaps a wild flower design would be a change from the usual roses.

Rosalind bent down to pick some bluebells and a stem of pink campion and a voice behind her said: "Lovely morning."

She straightened up, looking as startled and guilty as if she had been caught stealing a neighbour's prize tulips. It was rare to meet anybody on the footpath. Most people in Swallowfields got out their cars to cover the three miles to the next village.

"Yes, lovely," she said rather breathlessly, and one of the bluebells she was holding fell to the ground.

The tall man in the pale blue shirt that matched the colour of his eyes picked it up and gravely handed it to her.

"Thanks," said Rosalind. "It is Mr. Goodwin, isn't it? I heard your talk to the W.I. and I tried out one of your suggestions. The lemon balm as a sedative and tonic. It really worked."

"Did it?" He laughed. "That's a relief!"

Rosalind smiled too, beginning to feel more at ease. "Why, didn't you expect it to?" she asked.

"Shall I let you into a secret?" said Bernard Goodwin.

"That probably means you are going to tell me something that everyone else knows already," retorted Rosalind, "but yes, do go on. If it's something to do with plants I'll be very interested. I love them."

"And so do I, but I wish I hadn't started on this medicinal herb racket because in the first place I don't know enough about it and in the second place it's very dicey. I ought to have stuck to the old country customs and the modern farming methods. The farmers like a bit of good publicity and if people are inspired by one of my efforts to revive some idiotic medieval sport it won't do anyone any harm. But plants." He shook his head and prodded at the long grass with his stick. "They're the very devil. There's death in plants. What would you say was the name of this fine specimen of the Umbelliferae family, for instance?"

He stood there pointing with the stick and waited for Rosalind to answer. She felt rather like a schoolgirl being taken for a nature walk by the teacher. The intense emotional reaction to the beauty of the day had faded and she was rather enjoying the encounter. He was a very conceited man, she decided, as this sort of publicist usually was, but he was much better company than anybody she had yet met in the village.

"It looks like cow parsley," she said, glancing at the hedgerow at the spot where his stick was pointing.

"Ah." He sounded pleased, as if she were his prize pupil. "Cow parsley. Or Queen Anne's lace, as many people call it. One of the commonest of our wayside weeds. Of course you would say that and so would nine-hundred-and-ninety-nine people out of a thousand, if they were capable of giving a name to it at all. But it isn't, you know."

"It isn't cow parsley?" Rosalind looked again at the tall clump of spreading stems and creamy umbrella-like flower-heads. "Well, what is it then?" she added rather impatiently.

"Ah, now I have you guessing, my dear Mrs. Bannister. You see, I remember you too. You didn't think I did, did you?

You were casting me in the role of the self-centered successful man, too important to remember some modest little lady with whom he exchanged a few words at a Women's Institute meeting—and what condescension, what luck to get him to address such a meeting at all! That's what you were thinking, weren't you, Rosalind Bannister?"

"Well, yes. I suppose I was," admitted Rosalind.

"Then you'd better start revising your opinion. I am a very ordinary sort of schoolmaster who had two great strokes of luck that changed his life completely. One was the inheriting of a very welcome slice of money from an uncle and the other was to hit on a growth industry—writing and talking about the wonders of nature. That's all. I've been lucky and I've known how to use my luck. If we're going to be friends we'd better get that straight at once, just as you'd better stop this modest little woman act. That isn't you at all."

Rosalind took a deep breath before she replied. "I suppose somebody has told you," she said at last, "that I was acquitted of the manslaughter of my husband."

"Nobody told me, my dear. I read about it. Who didn't? Very brave of you to keep the name, if I may say so. It would have been even braver to go on being yourself instead of putting on an act."

"Mr. Goodwin—"

"Bernard, please."

"Mr. Goodwin, I don't think you can have any conception whatever of what life is like for a woman in my position. I dare not slip an inch. I am watched and studied and talked about and speculated over . . . It's like being in a goldfish tank. I am constantly on show. If I make the least mistake, if I show the slightest sign of temper or even mild irritation, if I drop the least hint of a violent reaction . . ."

Rosalind had started by speaking very firmly but her voice began to falter as she went on.

"I understand all that," interrupted Bernard Goodwin, "but I still think it is a mistake to try to impose a false personality upon oneself because the true one is always liable to break through, and it could be at a most inconvenient time."

There was a moment's silence and then Rosalind said in a

very bright and unnatural manner: "Thank you for your good advice. Perhaps you ought to be writing the agony column and not the country questions. Actually I thought we were talking about cow parsley."

"Ah yes, the ubiquitous weed that has strong medicinal virtues, according to one authority whom I have recently been consulting. A decoction of the leaves or the seeds or both is an excellent tonic, and also a diuretic. The roots are a good source of vitamins. It's only a carrot, you know. A wild carrot, as the French call it."

He continued to talk about the uses of cow parsley, while Rosalind recovered her balance. She was grateful for the chance to do so but at the same time she had the feeling of being manipulated by this comparative stranger and she was both resentful and rather afraid. There was a great deal of truth in what he had said; too much for her peace of mind, and she had the uneasy feeling that he knew a great deal about her, not only the history that everybody knew, but about herself as she was now. Since the only opportunities he had had to gain that knowledge were a short conversation on a public occasion and this present encounter, this meant that either he was a very perceptive sort of person or that she was giving herself away much more than she had thought.

"The wonders of nature," she said lightly when he came to a temporary pause in the lecture. "A whole chemist's shop in every hedgerow. Except that I thought you said this clump here was not cow parsley."

"That's right." He bent to pick a leaf, crushed it between his forefinger and thumb, and then held it out to Rosalind. "Take a sniff of that."

She looked at him suspiciously for a second or two before taking the crumpled piece of greenery. She liked wild flowers and enjoyed painting them, but she had no great botanical knowledge and had no idea what he was getting at. Whether he just wanted to show off his knowledge, or whether he had some particular reason for wanting to get to know her better she could not tell.

"What a revolting smell," she said, sniffing at the leaf. "It's like tomcats."

"Cat's piddle. Yes. Sorry to subject you to it, but it is much the best way to find out whether you are gathering the very useful Queen Anne's lace or whether you've got a piece of hemlock in your hand by mistake."

"Hemlock?" Rosalind stared at the plant with a new interest. "Is this really hemlock? I never knew it grew just like that. I mean, obviously it has to grow somewhere, but I rather thought . . ." She broke off and laughed a little. "How ignorant one is! I suppose I associated it with Socrates in ancient Greece and not with the English countryside!"

"It's quite a common plant," said Bernard, "and it likes the same sort of places as the cow parsley as well as being similar in appearance. Hence the danger."

"Is it really so very deadly?"

"Very. A notorious poisoner. I shouldn't lick your fingers if I were you."

Rosalind detected a note of mockery in his voice. The Mrs. Bannister that Swallowfields knew would have meekly replied, "Thank you for warning me." But the true Rosalind, who was revealing herself more and more in this conversation, could not resist rising to such a challenge.

"Tastes bitter, does it?" she said, and raised the crushed leaf to her lips.

A hand came up and caught her wrist. "I'm quite serious," said Bernard.

"Are you?" She looked up at him. "I thought this was some little game of yours."

Their eyes met and they were intensely aware of each other and Rosalind told herself in a panic that this was insane, that she must not get involved with any man at all in any capacity whatever, and least of all with one who was a public figure and who had a wife. To do that would be risking her whole future, a risk much greater, in all probability, than that of chewing on this evil-smelling leaf now. But at the very same moment that she knew she must keep away from this man who held such fascination for her she also knew that it was already too late.

The silence seemed to last for a long time. It was as if they were both mesmerized.

"Don't you believe me," said Bernard at last, "when I tell

you that you are holding a deadly poison? If you don't, you can always look it up in the encyclopedia. Or I'll lend you some books on toxic plants."

"Oh, I believe you all right," said Rosalind, pulling her hand away and letting the leaf fall to the ground. "The thing that's puzzling me is why you have gone out of your way to point out to me the properties of hemlock."

"Simple enough. You were obviously interested in herbal medicine. I could tell that at my lecture. And equally obviously you were a woman of character and persistence who would pursue an interest and not flit from one passing craze to another like most of them."

Rosalind resisted the temptation to ask how he could possibly have come to that conclusion in so short a time. Instead she said: "I was wondering whether you thought I might be interested in poisonous plants because I had killed my husband."

He appeared to give this remark serious consideration. They had moved on, by silent consent, and were walking side by side along the footpath, very close together because there was only just room for two between the hedgerow and the young green corn. At last he said: "You are partly right. I wanted to get to know you when I learned who you were, because I am very interested in people who have been through harrowing experiences and are in the position of having to re-create a life. I was once in that position myself. But I am certainly not warning you to keep off the poisoning because Big Brother is watching you. People who pick up the nearest weapon to get out of an intolerable situation are quite different from poisoners who work by stealth."

"Thank you," said Rosalind.

"But I did think," he went on, "that you might be capable of doing some harm to yourself. I reckoned you were just about coming up for the time when the anaesthetic after-effects of the experience would be wearing off—it seems to take up to a couple of years—and you would find yourself feeling intensely vulnerable again. And great loneliness combined with great sensitivity is one of the surest recipes for self-destruction."

"You were right," said Rosalind in a low voice. "How very strange that anybody else should understand."

"I told you I'd been through something similar. Quite a few years ago now. If we are going to be friends I'll tell you about it. Are we going to be friends, Rosalind?"

"I should like to be, but I really don't see how. In London it would be possible, and perhaps even in Brighton, but not in rural Sussex. Walls have ears and hedges have eyes. As far as we can see there is not a single other human being within view, but I'll bet you anything that when I get to our monthly meeting this evening there won't be a woman in that room who doesn't know that you and I have been walking in the country together this morning."

"A bet!" said Bernard, smiling broadly and looking almost as young as Rosalind herself. "I love a bet and I can see you are a natural gambler. But we don't want anything so crude as money. I've got plenty of it at the moment and you've probably got very little, so it would be embarrassing, because obviously I am going to win. What shall we wager?"

He stood still and Rosalind stood still with him. They were coming up to the spot where the footpath joined the road, and on the other side of the hedge cars were going by. A salutary reminder of the outside world intruding upon this rustic idyll. But the damage had already been done and she had been betrayed by the beauty of the morning into a genuine human contact again. It was with a feeling of apprehension mixed with elation that she said: "I've very little to offer. John had a life insurance that was just enough for me to buy the cottage, and Martin and I live on my pension and on the money I get from painting."

"Painting. Yes, I heard you were an artist. That's the bet then. If there is even one person—no more than one—at your W.I. meeting this evening who did not previously know that you and I met this morning, then you will do the illustrations for my book on the medicinal uses of common plants. It'll be quite well paid. My previous illustrator died recently and I have no doubt that my publishers will accept my recommendation."

"But this is ridiculous!" cried Rosalind. "If you want to offer me a job why don't you do it in the usual way?"

"Don't you think it's more amusing like this?"

"No, I don't. I think it's childish."

"That's because you're afraid you won't get the job. You needn't worry. You're going to lose the bet."

"But how . . . I mean suppose you lose it? What are you going to pay me?"

"That's a thought." He had begun to walk on and now stopped again. "Where does your son go to school?"

"He's been going in to Brighton every day. What's that got to do with it?"

"How does he get there?"

"Bus, of course."

"Then I'll buy him a motor-bike. Every parent's nightmare, so I'm told," he added, seeing Rosalind's instant look of alarm. "I wouldn't know about it myself, never having had any children."

Rosalind took a deep breath and a firm grip on herself. It was time to stop all this nonsense, once and for all.

"Look, Mr. Goodwin—" she began.

"Bernard."

"All right then. Christian names mean nothing nowadays. Look, Bernard, don't you think we'd better forget all this talk about bets and personal experiences and just stick to the nature study? We met in the fields and you gave me a lecture on wild flowers but apart from that you and I are just as we were before this morning."

He made no reply but simply smiled and shook his head while Rosalind looked at him appealingly.

"Anyway," she said, feeling defeated and suspecting that there was rather a peevish note in her voice, "there's no means of knowing who has won this stupid bet. You won't be at the meeting this evening and I'm certainly not going to go round to everybody in the room in turn and say I met Bernard Goodwin when I was out walking this morning and did you know about it."

"You wouldn't get a truthful answer if you did, but you'll know all right, and I'll just have to trust to your honour to let me know the outcome. If I don't hear about it from another source, of course."

"I wish to God I'd never come out this morning," said Rosalind despairingly.

"Cheer up," said Bernard, pulling open the gate into the road. "You're bound to gain either way. A nice job for you or a nice bike for your boy. What are you worrying about, woman?"

He went through the gate, closed it behind him, and waved at her. "You've lost your bluebells. You'll have to pick some more," he said before walking briskly off along the road.

2

The speaker for that evening's meeting was Rosalind's friend
Lesley Green, who was going to show slides and talk about her
holiday in Egypt the previous winter. Everybody, including
Miss Green herself, knew that this sort of talk was always a
makeshift, brought in if a speaker had let them down at the last
minute or if it had been impossible to get the one they wanted.
The members of the Swallowfields branch rather prided
themselves on being intelligent women, who were interested in
the big questions of the day and not just a local gossip shop and
recipe-exchange centre.

Outwardly regrets were expressed that the speaker originally
asked for was unable to come, but most of the women in the
room were privately quite relieved to sit looking at Lesley
Green's colourful pictures and not to have to struggle with the
complexities of the forthcoming elections to the European
Parliament. Other peoples' holiday photographs could, of
course, be terribly boring, but most people who lived in
Swallowfields had enough money to go to places slightly off
the package holiday tracks and enough liveliness of mind to get
the most out of them. So they tolerated each other's experiences very well, either when presented in private houses or
publicly in the village hall.

Lesley Green was the most reliable of all the standbys, a
wiry little grey-haired woman with a brisk manner and an
authoritative voice that had in the past kept generations of

noisy schoolchildren under control. She never over-ran her time; her anecdotes were always amusing; and since she worked the projector herself you could be quite sure that there would be none of those irritating hold-ups and breakdowns in the actual showing of the slides.

Rosalind sat in the back row near the door. It was a modern building, purpose-built as a community centre, with big picture windows and a fine view of the distant South Downs which it was a pity to have to black out on this light summer evening. The business part of the meeting had already begun and the Treasurer was telling her usual tale of woe when Rosalind heard the sound of footsteps on the polished wooden floor behind her and a moment later somebody slipped into the empty chair next to her at the end of the row. She waited for a few seconds before giving a sideways glance and in that short space of time she had an overwhelming impression of some-body in a great state of nervous tension. So strong was this feeling of anxiety and unease that it had an almost physical presence like a scent or a current of air.

Rosalind turned her head and smiled at the newcomer. She was a woman of about Rosalind's own age, possibly a little younger, wearing a simple cream-coloured dress that showed off her classic beauty. The hair was auburn and the skin was good and the eyes a fascinating and unusual shade of green, and yet it was not her striking looks but her anxiety that made the greater impression on Rosalind, who could never see or sense any sort of distress without at the same time feeling an overwhelming urge to take action to try to ease it.

"You haven't missed much," she whispered, putting into her voice and her smile all the comfort and reassurance that she could command in the circumstances. "They're only arguing about how much to charge for coffee."

The auburn-haired woman achieved a faint smile. It did not improve her looks; there was too much contempt in it.

"Typical women's meeting," she said. Then she quickly added, as if sensing that she was not making too good an impression: "D'you mind my sitting here? I like to feel I can get out quickly. I get claustrophobia in a room full of people."

"So do I," said Rosalind. "I always try to stay at the back."

A heated argument had now developed at the front of the hall between the Treasurer and a dark youngish woman who looked rather overheated herself in jeans and a woollen sweater on this warm evening. Most of the other women in the room seemed to want to express an opinion on the matter under discussion and the meeting got rather out of control. Under cover of the general noise Rosalind talked more comfortably to her neighbour.

"I haven't seen you before, have I?" she said. "Are you on a visit here?"

"No, I live here. I moved down with my husband a little while ago."

Rosalind's mind began to run over the names of people whom she knew to be comparatively new arrivals to the village and a suspicion began to form. It was confirmed a moment later.

"I'm Jane Goodwin," said the newcomer. "My husband is a writer and broadcaster. He gave a talk to you a little while back which I ought to have come to but didn't."

"I suppose you didn't feel able to sit in a crowded meeting," said Rosalind sympathetically. "I can well understand that."

"Can you?" Again there was that flash of contempt in the green eyes. "Yes, I dare say you can. You're Mrs. Bannister, aren't you?"

There was still a certain nervousness in the voice, but also a strong curiosity, and Rosalind felt the still sensitive core of herself recoil as she replied that she was.

"I spoke to your husband after his lecture," she said. "Perhaps he mentioned me to you."

"He said you'd be here tonight. Otherwise I wouldn't have come."

At this moment the altercation at the front of the hall suddenly ceased and Miss Lesley Green was called upon to begin her talk. There was no possibility of any further conversation and after a moment's reflection Rosalind felt glad of this because she badly needed time in which to adjust her ideas. Under cover of the story of the voyage up the Nile, which had most of the audience frequently breaking out into laughter, Rosalind mentally took stock. So this is Bernard's wife, she thought, whom we have all been so curious about but whom few of us have ever seen, let alone got to know. Good-looking enough, but in a bad way at the moment. Some sort of temporary nervous illness? Or a permanent condition? Drugs? Alcohol?

Whatever it was, there was certainly something very wrong with Jane Goodwin, which explained why she had up till now taken no part in the life of the village, and why Bernard had said very little about her except that she was not very well at the moment. But if she really was nervous of meeting people, wouldn't it have been more sensible to start with inviting one or two people to the house, rather than come to a meeting of this kind, always a bit of an ordeal even to a non-nervous person?

"I only came to meet you," Jane had said.

Why was that? Sheer curiosity to see the notorious Mrs. Bannister in the flesh? Rosalind found it hard to believe this. For all her present tension, Jane looked a sophisticated sort of woman who must surely have met plenty of people who had been in the public eye for one reason or another. To see someone who had been charged with killing her husband would not be of such importance that she would subject herself to sitting through a lecture in a public hall. Was she then keen to meet Rosalind because of what Bernard had told her? That didn't seem to make sense either until Rosalind suddenly remembered that absurd bet, which had been in and out of her mind all day but that had been pushed into the background during her short conversation with Bernard's wife.

Now she put the two together—the bet and the meeting with Jane—and everything slipped into place. Jane Goodwin did not mix in village society; she would certainly not know that Rosalind had talked with her husband in the fields that morning. That was why Bernard had been so sure that he was going to win his bet. He had determined to get Jane to the meeting so that there would be the essential one person there who didn't know. How he had persuaded her Rosalind could not guess, but evidently meeting Rosalind had been held out as some sort of bait.

Why?

Rosalind puzzled over this for the rest of the lecture, and she also puzzled over the fact that Bernard obviously wanted her to meet Jane for the first time on neutral ground, so to speak. The nearest she could get to an explanation of it all was that Bernard wanted a friend for his wife, a friend who, judging by Jane's condition, would have to do a great deal of reassuring and supporting. In other words, Rosalind had been chosen from among the other women of the village to be a sort of psychiatric nurse to Bernard's difficult wife. That was what it looked like, and to think that she, Rosalind Bannister, aged forty-four and not exactly inexperienced in the ways of men and women, had actually believed for a moment that Bernard had been attracted to herself!

You're a fool, Ros, she said to herself: that'll teach you to go imagining that you still have any charms for any man. Fortunately there was no harm done, however, because she was not in the slightest danger of falling in love with him, good company though he was and good-looking too in a rather hawklike manner. She might be superficially attracted, but she would never become seriously emotionally involved with such a conceited and double-dealing sort of man. Jane Goodwin would have to cope with her troubles without Rosalind's help, and as for that silly bet, if Bernard became troublesome Rosalind believed she knew how to deal with him. The great thing in life was to see clearly what people were up to: that always gave you the advantage.

Firm in this resolution, Rosalind sat through the rest of the lecture, vaguely aware of Lesley Green's high clear voice and the succession of colourful images that flashed on the screen.

". . . however much we complain about the evils of the age in which we live," said Lesley, "it's always a relief to step back into the last quarter of the twentieth century after living in the past . . ."

As she was speaking, the picture changed from a pyramid silhouetted against an evening sky to an airliner shining white against the brilliant blue of noon and it was obvious that the talk was drawing to an end. Rosalind became aware that the woman beside her was shifting restlessly in her chair.

"I'm getting out," she whispered, "before the lights come on. Don't want to meet any of this dreary gang."

True to her resolution, Rosalind made no reply, but during the subsequent burst of clapping, and while the hall was still in darkness, she had a sudden revulsion of feeling. Jane Goodwin could hardly be blamed for her husband's schemes, and had it been anybody else who had slipped away like that Rosalind would have got up to follow to see whether they were all right. Just this once, she said to herself as she quickly made her way out of the hall. She really is in a bad state, and I can't let her go without making sure at least that she will get home safely.

Jane had passed through the foyer and the main door of the building and was standing at the bottom of the short flight of steps. She was clearly visible in the light that shone through the open door, and the tension in her was equally plain.

Rosalind came down the steps and touched her arm.

"How are you getting home?" she asked.

Jane gave a start and then spoke in a bright artificial voice that held a note of hysteria.

"Oh hullo! Have you had enough too? Ghastly bore, holiday photos, aren't they? And women's organizations. Too frightful for words."

"Well, that's village society," said Rosalind mildly. "It can be quite pleasant if you take it in the right spirit."

She had not intended this as any sort of reproof and was rather appalled when Jane suddenly burst out sobbing.

"That's what my husband says," she gasped. "He gets furious with me."

She produced a handkerchief and blew her nose before continuing in a somewhat calmer voice.

"It's not only that I'm rather a snob and I do find women *en masse* boring," she said. "It's mainly this awful thing of mine about being among a lot of people. It's one of the reasons we moved out of London and my husband thought I'd be better here but I seem to be as bad as ever."

The voice rose again, threatening a further outburst.

"How long have you been like this?" asked Rosalind.

"About eight years. On and off. Sometimes it's worse. Sometimes it nearly goes. Ever since the accident."

Accident, thought Rosalind. Would that be the traumatic event in his own past at which Bernard had hinted? Aloud she said: "Is it just the being in a room with other people? Or does it affect you in other ways as well?"

"When it's very bad," cried Jane, anger and resentment now swamping the anxiety in her, "it affects me in every bloody way you can think of. I can't be in the streets, I can't go into a shop or a restaurant or a theatre or on a train or on a plane. I can't do anything. It's like—it's like . . ."

Words failed her. She was speechless from fury.

"It's like being under house arrest, like being a prisoner in your own home. Yes, I know," said Rosalind.

"How do you know?" demanded Jane aggressively. "You can't possibly know. You're running around leading a perfectly normal life."

"Yes, I am now. More or less," said Rosalind, with some difficulty controlling her increasing irritation with Jane Goodwin. "But I was in exactly the condition you describe when they finally decided that I was not guilty of the manslaughter of my husband. I was perfectly free physically but my mind was in prison. I couldn't bear to go out of the flat and I couldn't bear anybody to visit me. I sent Martin out to do the shopping and any other errands and got him to do all the talking on the phone. Poor Martin. He had a terrible time. As if he hadn't had a bad enough time already. I had lots of tranquillizers and sedatives and various kinds of psychiatric treatment but it wasn't until it came home to me what I was doing to my son that I managed to pull out of it and I only get mild attacks nowadays. I can remember exactly what it feels like, though, and I must say I think it was very brave of you to come to the meeting this evening."

"Bernard more or less threw me into it," said Jane with a short harsh laugh. "He'll be collecting me soon. We said half past nine. Don't let him know I came out early," she added, catching hold of Rosalind by the arm and giving her a little shake.

She's afraid of him, thought Rosalind; even more afraid of him at this moment than of her own fear. I wonder why?

"Of course I won't," she said, "but don't you think it's better not to pretend? It only makes you even more tense and more resentful too, if you pretend not to be anxious when in fact you are."

Jane laughed again, even more bitterly than before. "Depends who you live with, doesn't it?" she said. "You seem to have plenty of sympathy at home. I haven't."

"I suppose," said Rosalind, very carefully because this was treading on dangerous ground, quite apart from the fact that she was now beginning to dislike Jane very much indeed, "that it is not all that easy, living with somebody who is subject to fears of this sort. I think one has to try to see the other person's point of view, however bad one feels."

"You're bloody right it isn't easy. According to my dear delightful husband it's he who's the one to be pitied. A man in his position, always in demand all over the place, he needs a wife who's a social asset, doesn't he? A good hostess, a good mixer. Intelligent but not too much so. Well-dressed and also good-looking if possible. Okay, so he's got the last two, that's all. And when I'm really bad I can't even be bothered to make up properly and I look like hell."

Jane was speaking very loudly now. Rosalind glanced back at the entrance to the hall and was relieved to see no sign of anybody else coming out yet.

"Oh yes, poor old Bernie's got a rotten bargain," cried Jane, "particularly when you think what a price he paid for it! The wonder is that he's put up with it so long. I'm expecting any day—" and she began to sob again—"that he'll decide it's time to get rid of me too."

"Might it not be better," said Rosalind even more cautiously than before, "I mean, if it's as difficult as all that, wouldn't you have more chance of recovering if you were on your own, without the strain of keeping up appearances for somebody else? Have you ever considered a separation or even a divorce?"

It was said very gently and tactfully, but even so it provoked a violent reaction.

"Divorce!" exclaimed Jane. "Bernie doesn't hold with divorce. Not on any moral grounds. Oh no. We're a communicant member of the Church of England, we are, but we don't inconvenience ourselves with things like morals. We don't like divorce because it's untidy, that's all. It leaves loose ends. It has disagreeable after-effects, like having to pay out large sums in alimony, for example. Oh no. Bernie isn't thinking about divorce. It's murder that he's got in mind."

It was Rosalind's turn to be startled, but she quickly brought herself under control again, reflecting that Jane was now in a thoroughly hysterical condition and talking quite wildly. It would be very unwise to take seriously anything that she said. This was not the moment to try to give her any advice and the only thing to be done now was to calm her down as much as possible before Bernard arrived, which could happen at any moment.

"Let's go and wait in the road," said Rosalind, ignoring Jane's outburst. "It'll save your husband having to turn into the car park. And it'll also save us from the general exodus from the meeting," she added, seeing that the idea of saving Bernard trouble had no appeal for Jane.

"What a perfect evening," she went on as they walked across the tarmac. "I love this moment just before it gets dark and the whole sky looks like sapphires and the trees are jet black against it."

Jane made no reply, but Rosalind had hardly expected any, and they stood in silence under the streetlamp at the entrance to the car park until a white car came round the corner from the High Street. It was a smallish Renault, not the least bit showy, and Rosalind was rather surprised. She would have expected Bernard to drive something more impressive, but perhaps this was why he chose it: to surprise people in just this manner.

He drew up alongside them, got out of the car, and greeted Rosalind, with scarcely a glance at Jane.

"It's Mrs. Bannister, isn't it?" he said. "We talked about lemon balm as a sedative for overworked minds. Did you ever try it?"

Rosalind was taken off guard. She should have been ready for Bernard to pretend they had not met since the day of his lecture but she was not.

"Well, as a matter of fact—" she began feebly and was relieved when he interrupted her.

"Have you been looking after my little wife for me? Has she been behaving herself?"

The tone of this remark and the manner in which it was uttered stung Rosalind into sympathy for Jane again.

"We both decided to come out before the end of the meeting," she said in a very matter-of-fact voice, "because it was hot and stuffy in the hall and we needed a breath of air. Since then we've been having an interesting conversation."

Rosalind had learned enough about Jane Goodwin during their brief acquaintance not to expect any gratitude for championing her and she was not surprised when Jane abruptly let go of her arm to which she had been clinging, stepped towards the car, and snapped at her husband: "Come on. Let's get out of here."

"Not so fast," said Bernard, barring her way. "Say goodnight nicely to Mrs. Bannister like a good girl."

Rosalind spoke quickly before Jane could say anything. It looked as though another fit of hysteria was on the way, and Rosalind was determined to prevent it if possible and at the same time to show up Bernard's pretence.

"Goodnight, Mrs. Goodwin," she said. "I'm very glad to have met you and I hope we will meet again. You've very welcome to drop in on me any time you are in the village. And by the way, I meant to tell you while we were talking but I didn't get the chance. I met your husband out walking along the Leahurst footpath this morning and he gave me a long lecture on the difference between hemlock and cow parsley, both growing along the hedges there. I thought you might be interested to know this."

As she said these words Rosalind glanced first at Bernard and then at Jane. Their faces showed up clearly in the light of the streetlamp. In Bernard's face Rosalind thought she caught a glimpse of anger, quickly brought under control. The effect on Jane was more dramatic. Her whole body began to shake and she gave a loud screech of laughter.

"Hemlock!" she cried, the painful laugh coming once more. "Is that what it's going to be? Like Socrates. Stupid Jane, the bird brain, is going to die like the great philosopher. Oh, that's funny! That's absolutely killing!"

Her voice died away into gasping, sobbing laughter.

Bernard caught hold of her arm and pushed her into the car. Then he turned to Rosalind and said quite calmly and politely: "I suppose you think you know everything now and I suppose it is quite useless to assure you that you are wrong."

Rosalind met his eye equally steadily. "I don't suppose that I know anything whatever," she said, "except that your wife is in a highly nervous condition at this moment. It would be very difficult not to realize that, but I don't presume to have any notion of the reason for it."

Again they looked at each other. Jane's sobbing could be heard from the car, and a sudden loud burst of voices showed that the meeting in the village hall had broken up at last.

Bernard inclined his head slightly. "I am glad you do me that much justice," he said. "Will you do me the further justice of hearing my side of the story at the first convenient opportunity, since I must take it that you have heard the other side?"

"I don't think it would be advisable for us to meet any more," said Rosalind.

"I see. You are determined to take Jane's side. I suppose I risked that when I contrived this meeting, but it did seem to me best that you should first meet on neutral ground and it also seemed to me that a woman with your particular experience would not be so quick to condemn on hearsay evidence as most unthinking people might be."

Rosalind felt the blood surge to her cheeks and she could no longer restrain her indignation. "To remind me at this moment," she burst out.

"Not very gentlemanly, I admit, but I've never pretended to be a gentleman. I'm a self-made man and proud of it. I'm also rather desperate at this moment and I believe you could help me."

Rosalind glanced across the car park to the still brightly lit village hall. A group of women were walking towards the entrance gates, talking loudly and cheerfully. In a very few seconds they would be at the spot where the white Renault stood and whatever was going on between Bernard and Jane Goodwin and Rosalind Bannister would be public property in Swallowfields. Rosalind felt trapped, and the sensation was made peculiarly intense and horrible by the memory of her own time of trial.

"All right then," she said in desperation. "Come and talk to me if you must. But you're to tell your wife that you're coming, or else I'll tell her myself. I'm not having any more of this concealment."

Bernard made a little bow. "Thank you," he said. "I'll be with you tomorrow morning at about half past ten if that's convenient, and I assure you that Jane will know about it."

"Good night then," said Rosalind abruptly and strode off down the road. She had just turned the corner into the High Street when the group of women reached Bernard's car and the loud cries of recognition and delight reached Rosalind's ears as she hurried to the sanctuary of her cottage.

— 3 —

Rosalind's home was at the end of a small terrace of cottages near the church. A white wooden gate opened on to a tiny flagged courtyard and the entrance to the house was at the side. The living-room was at the back; the kitchen and its tiny adjoining scullery that Rosalind used as a studio had windows overlooking the courtyard in front, and both of these were showing lights when Rosalind shut the gate. In the kitchen she rescued a pan of milk that was just about to boil over on the gas cooker and in the studio she found Martin leaning over a painting that had reached a rather delicate stage. Crumbs were on the point of falling on to it from the bread and butter that he was eating and Rosalind leapt forward to whisk away the drawing-board.

"All right. No harm done," she said a moment later. "Hullo, darling. What was the milk for?"

"Milk." Martin ate some more bread and butter and appeared to consider this. "Oh, yes. Milk. It just seemed a good idea to boil some. Chocolate, I think. Yes. Chocolate. Something filling."

"I'll have some too," said Rosalind. "I missed the refreshments this evening."

"All this gadding about," said Martin, taking a couple of mugs off the draining-board. "All this wild social life. It won't do, Mum, you know. It won't do at all. You're turning me into a latchkey kid."

"Haven't you had a meal?" she asked a few minutes later. They were sitting by the open living-room window, looking out into the scented dimness of the garden, and Martin was starting on a third slice of bread and butter.

"Well, not really, I suppose," he replied. "We had orchestra rehearsal and Deirdre did suggest that I should go back to her place afterwards but I've had three dinners there already this week and I don't want her to think I just look on her as a free meal ticket."

This was said in Martin's normally cheerful manner, without the slightest trace of bitterness or self-pity, but it caused Rosalind a sudden intense pain that she had hard work to conceal. Deirdre Parker was the only child of a prosperous local solicitor who had built a luxury bungalow on the outskirts of Brighton, where he had his practice, and she sat next to Martin among the second violins in the school orchestra. Rosalind liked both the girl and her parents, whom she had met at a concert, and she was sure that they did not object to their daughter's friendship with Martin, as some parents might have done, because he had a mother who had once been in the news headlines. But the style of living at Deirdre's home was very different from that at No. 1 Church Cottages, and Martin would be more than human if he did not sometimes feel sensitive about it. It was also hardly possible that eighteen-year-old human nature should not sometimes feel hard done by to have had an adolescence like Martin's.

The years of struggling to keep up the appearance of a successful literary household, while Martin's father turned from a normal social drinker into a heavy drinker and then went right over the edge as his strength of will and his talents failed him and his manuscripts were rejected and his debts mounted higher and higher; and then those last nightmarish months when self-pity turned to violence, which awoke an answering violence in Martin, then fifteen years old and tough and tall for his age and very like his father in appearance; and Rosalind, forced into the position of keeping them apart, had found within herself springs of violence whose existence she had never suspected until that time.

It had been anybody's guess, those last months, which one

of the three of them would finally do the irreparable damage. When Rosalind had flung that hammer it had been to stop an exceptionally vicious fight between her husband and her son. She had had no intention of hitting either of them, but had aimed at the wall above and behind them in order to frighten them both into some self-control. She was a good shot and had been a better bowler than her two elder brothers in family games of cricket on the lawn of the Old Rectory years ago. The hammer had been to hand because they had all been in the kitchen, where Martin was repairing a cupboard door, when the balloon went up. She had mentally marked the spot on the wall at which she was aiming, but unfortunately she had not noticed that the head of the hammer was loose. It came away from the handle in its flight and found a nearer target—John Bannister's right temple, killing him instantly.

Rosalind and Martin never talked about that moment now, nor about the months that followed it. They lived in the present and in the future, but every now and then the memory of the past would come up and give one or the other of them a sharp unexpected blow, like that deflected hammer-blow, and on these occasions the first thought of each was always to conceal the suffering from the other.

"I don't suppose Deirdre's mother would mind how many meals you eat there," said Rosalind. "From what I saw of her I should guess that she's only too delighted to have people enjoy her cooking, but I know what you mean, all the same. I'll make you an omelette. Mushroom or cheese or tomato?"

"Tomato, please. Thanks, Mum."

"I don't know why you didn't ask straight away instead of doing this martyred act," grumbled Rosalind as she went into the kitchen.

"I thought you'd be too exhausted with your festivities to want to start cooking when you came in," retorted Martin.

"My festivities," said Rosalind, "my rave-ups at the Women's Institute meetings, have gone and got me into a bit of a dilemma and I want your advice."

This was a sure way to cheer Martin up, if indeed he needed any cheering. He loved giving advice at any time, and towards his mother he was particularly protective.

"A proposal of marriage!" he exclaimed. "A suitor! Two suitors and you've got to choose between them. Tell me all."

"It's nothing like that, you idiot. It's much more complicated. I've gone and got myself involved in somebody else's matrimonial problems. God knows I didn't want to, but I was positively dragged into it."

"Whose?" asked Martin with his mouth full.

"The Goodwins. I told you about Bernard Goodwin."

"Oh yes. The naturalist in Sussex. Balmy Bernard. He's done very well for himself. D'you think I ought to have taken botany instead of chemistry and physics, Mum?"

"No, I don't. You can't tell a daffodil from a dandelion. I'll never ask you to weed the garden again, so you've saved yourself that chore. I never knew anybody could be so hopeless as you are about identifying plants. That's how it all started, by the way. I met Bernard Goodwin on the footpath to Leahurst this morning and he explained to me the difference between cow parsley and hemlock."

"Hemlock? The stuff they gave Socrates?"

"Yes, and I'm getting just a little bit tired of Socrates. Now listen, Martin."

"I'm all ears."

Rosalind gave him an edited account of her conversation with Bernard, leaving in the suggestion of some dramatic happening in his own past, but leaving out the bet and saying simply that he had mentioned that he could get her the job of illustrating his current book if she was interested.

"But that would be super," interrupted Martin. "If you could get a foot into book illustration you'd soon be going places."

"Yes, I know it's very tempting, but I'm not sure I'd want to do it this way."

"Why? Didn't you like him?"

This was asked very casually, but Rosalind knew that they were now getting to the crux of the matter, and that Martin's peace of mind depended very much upon her reply.

"I can't say I actually disliked him," she said. "He's a lot more interesting to talk to than most of the people in Swallowfields. But after having met his wife at the W.I. meeting this evening, I can't help wishing that I'd never met either of them and that I didn't have to have anything more to do with them."

And she proceeded to describe the meeting with Jane and the encounter with Bernard in the car park, still doing a little editing, but not so much as for the morning's talk.

"Now *she* really does sound balmy," said Martin. "D'you think she was making it all up or is she really afraid he's going to kill her?"

"I don't know," said Rosalind slowly. "I didn't like her, but that shouldn't influence me. She was certainly very frightened, not only with this phobia of people that I had so badly myself for a time, but also frightened of him. And the way he spoke to her was rather beastly—a sort of condescending contempt. If that's the way he treats her when other people are present, I dread to think what he's like when they are alone."

There was a moment of silence while both their minds were occupied with the memory of what John Bannister had been like when nobody outside the family had been present, but neither of them referred to it aloud. Then Rosalind's mind slid on to the thought that she was deliberately making Bernard out to be worse than he really was in order to conceal from Martin her own fascination with him. Whether Martin was taken in by this or not she could not tell.

"I don't see how you can possibly judge whether she's got good cause to be afraid of him," said Martin at last, "until you know more about it. And you won't know that until you've heard his story. When is he coming?"

"Tomorrow morning."

"Would you like me to eavesdrop? If I stay here in the kitchen and you leave both doors open I'll be able to hear it all. Or I could lie on the lawn just under the living-room window."

"Don't be silly, Martin. You'll be at school."

"I won't, you know. Not Saturday morning."

"Good Lord, is it really Saturday?"

Martin looked at his watch. "Well, to be precise, it's exactly forty-three minutes away from being Saturday. Come on, Mum. Do let me eavesdrop. How can I advise you if I don't know what's happening? It'll save you having to repeat the whole thing to me later on."

Rosalind did not immediately reply. One part of her was

dreading meeting Bernard again, but another part of her, that part that threatened her self-control when she listened to Mozart or walked in the fields on a June morning, was looking forward to the morning and telling her that it was not just a vain delusion, that Bernard really was attracted to her for herself alone and not just as somebody who would help him cope with Jane.

But these were feelings that she must at all costs keep from Martin. He had gulped down and digested the appalling tragedy of his father, whom he had worshipped when he was a little boy, and he was tackling his own life with great courage. The last thing he needed was for his mother to become involved with another man in any way at all, whether that man was free or whether married, unhappily or not. Martin might joke about suitors, but Rosalind knew that he dreaded her marrying again more than he dreaded anything else in the world. Not only that, but he dreaded her showing any interest at all in any other man. If she were to become friendly with Bernard, and it was alarming how her mind persisted in scampering after this possibility in spite of what had happened that evening, then it could only be because she was primarily a friend of his wife's. Martin might just be able to cope with that. On the other hand, she had told him, perfectly truthfully, that she did not like Bernard's wife.

"I'd much rather have heard Jane's side of the story first," she said aloud, knowing that she had been silent for too long and that Martin would be becoming suspicious.

"Why? D'you think she's more likely to tell the truth than he is?"

Rosalind thought this over for a moment. "Not that exactly. But she is probably not as clever as he is and therefore probably not so good at lying."

"You think he's a liar, then," said Martin, "but you still like him?"

They were washing up now, and Rosalind was glad to be bending over the sink so that Martin could not see her face clearly. He was very observant at all times, and particularly sensitive to her own changes of mood and expression. That he did not like the idea of her having a *tête-à-tête* with Bernard

Goodwin was very clear to Rosalind. The suggestion of eavesdropping had been made in fun but it had a serious content as well. How was she to reassure him that he need not worry about Bernard, when he was capable of picking up the slightest hint of insincerity? In the end she decided that the best thing was to come out with the truth. At this stage it was innocent enough to cause Martin no great distress.

"I don't exactly like him, darling," she said, turning round so that he could see her face under the full glare of the strip lighting, "but I've got to confess that there's something about him that rather appeals to me. He's got a sort of cynical man of the world air that sets me wondering. And he can certainly lay on the charm. Even if you know he's laying it on, it still works. Yes, I do find him attractive as I dare say most women do, of all ages and types." She laughed. "I can't help it. It's a sort of chemical reaction. Do I like him? It depends on the circumstances. As the husband of an unhappy woman I don't like him at all. I think he is unspeakable. As a man who is trying to manipulate me for some reason of his own I don't like him either. As a writer and lecturer and an expert on flora and fauna I both like and admire him, and as an acquaintance to talk to at a party or other social gathering I think I should like him very much. There you are, darling. It was quite hard work thinking all that out, and it's only brought us back to what I said at first. I think I'm ready for bed now."

Martin made no comment, but he came and put his arms round her and laid his head down on her shoulder. This sort of demonstration of affection was rare with him and Rosalind knew that it meant he was both grateful to her and reassured about her attitude towards Bernard Goodwin. She held him for a moment and then moved away and said: "I honestly don't think it's a good idea to eavesdrop. It would be very embarrassing if he suddenly discovered you, but you can sit in on the interview if you like."

"That would be useless. If I'm there he'll either give a lecture or talk about the weather. In any case I promised to help Deirdre with a sponsored swim. I'd forgotten for the moment. Can I bring her back to lunch?"

"Of course. I'd love to see her."

"It's her birthday next week," said Martin, "and I was rather wondering . . ."

He had no need to finish the sentence. Mother and son were back on the same wavelength again, knowing each other's thoughts even before they were uttered.

"You'd like her to have a flower painting," said Rosalind. "That's why you were dropping crumbs all over my bluebells."

"Well, yes. I would rather. Preferably one of those oval ones. I'll pay you for it, of course."

"Of course you will. If you want a free gift for your girlfriend you can make it yourself. I'll put a selection out for her to choose from. Okay, Martin?"

"Okay, Mum. Thanks."

4

That Martin went to bed happy and with his mind at peace had to be Rosalind's comfort too, because her own thoughts were far from restful and the blackbirds and thrushes were greeting the dawn before she slept at last. When Martin brought her tea, as he always did at the weekend, she came suddenly out of a nightmare and saw his face as that of his father. The impression lingered on even after she was fully awake and gave a feeling of shadowy unreality to the bright summer morning, as if she herself were slightly feverish.

When Bernard arrived she had only just returned from shopping. "I shan't be long," she said, pushing open the door of the living-room. "Find yourself something to read. Or go in to the garden if you like."

She was conscious of a strong desire to convey to him that his visit was only a minor incident in her own active day, of no more importance than a gossip with her neighbour, and at the same time she knew that he saw through this pretence.

"Did you manage to find somewhere to park?" she asked when she brought in the coffee tray and found him standing staring out of the window. "Saturday mornings are usually pretty hopeless in the village."

"I'm in the entrance to the churchyard," he replied as he sat down. "If there's a wedding or a funeral they'll have to tow me away."

"You could have gone a bit further along Church Lane,"

said Rosalind in the same formal and impersonal manner, "and parked opposite the police house. Arthur wouldn't have minded. He always winks at minor offences, and he's not at all in favour of yellow-lining Church Lane, which I gather they are going to do."

"You come out of London," said Bernard in the same manner, "to rural Sussex, thinking you've left traffic problems behind you, and you find the whole place is in the monstrous grip of the automobile too. Oh well. At least it has one great advantage."

He stopped to take a drink of coffee and Rosalind felt obliged to ask what the advantage was.

"Conversationally," said Bernard beaming at her, "the motor-car is just about the greatest asset that man ever devised. Carefully conserved, it can last an ill-assorted gathering of people for an entire evening. And it is a far better topic of conversation than the weather for people who are frightened of going down the steep slope into genuine personal encounter and are looking for an escape route."

"I'm not looking for an escape route," cried Rosalind with annoyance. "I'm only trying to get my breath back after doing my chores."

"Ah yes, the burden of a house to look after. I hear a lot about that at home."

He continued to beam at her but Rosalind made no reply. One slip-up was enough. From now on it was to be rigid self-control.

"You are no doubt thinking what a heartless way to talk about a sick woman," he continued presently, "and my behaviour to Jane is abominable, I admit. So is hers to me, in a more subtle and less obvious way. No, don't ask why don't we part then," he went on as Rosalind was about to put this very question, "because it is not as simple as that. We are linked together by bonds of guilt and hatred that are harder to break than any legal contract. Suppose when you threw that weapon it had killed or injured your son and not your husband, as it might so well have done. Would you and your husband ever have been able to part?"

Rosalind had gone very pale while he spoke. She herself was

only too well aware that it could have been Martin and not his father who was the victim of the accident, but to hear it put into words by somebody else was very disturbing.

"No, of course you wouldn't," said Bernard watching her closely. "It might have shocked John Bannister out of his drinking but that wouldn't have freed either of you. You'd have been clamped together in hell. As Jane and I are. Because that is our story, more or less. She's an alcoholic too, by the way."

"Do you mean that you were responsible—one or the other or both of you—for the death of your first wife?"

Rosalind was glad to find that her voice was steady. She was still feeling very shaken, both by Bernard's remark about Martin and by the effortless way in which he had demolished all her attempts to hold aloof and remain emotionally uninvolved.

"That's it," said Bernard. "The traumatic experience I mentioned yesterday morning. It was a car crash about eight years ago. It didn't make the headlines like your little affair, my dear Rosalind, partly because it was such a commonplace everyday sort of happening and partly because I was not so well known at that time as I am now. Not so well known as John Bannister at the time of his death. There were three of us in that car. My first wife, Glenda, myself, and Jane who was my part-time secretary."

"Nothing but your secretary?"

"Naturally she was not just my secretary. We were having an affair. How can one have a secretary like Jane and not be having an affair? That would be too much to ask. Particularly as Glenda and I had no more interest in each other and were sticking together for domestic convenience rather than for any other reason. We had a very nice flat in the Bloomsbury area at an incredibly low rent, and since a good home in Central London nowadays is even more beyond price than a good wife, neither of us wanted to budge. Glenda was a social worker and politically active in a different direction from myself. I was still teaching a bit but was beginning to make a name in my present line of country. The flat was big enough for us to go our separate ways. Glenda didn't mind Jane. She had her equivalent compensations. But Jane minded Glenda. She was not a particularly efficient secretary but she had social ambitions. She did another part-time job working for a bright young experimental psychologist who has since become notorious—I name no names—and he was her first choice. That didn't come off and she fell back on the hope of becoming Mrs. Bernard Goodwin. Are you looking disapproving, Rosalind? What is it that upsets you? My apparent callousness towards Jane? Or the fact that Glenda and I were leading our separate sinful lives in what is so quaintly known as the matrimonial home? It is not an unusual situation, I assure you."

"I didn't realize I was looking disapproving," said Rosalind. "I don't feel it. If anything, I'm just feeling rather sorry for you all."

"You would," said Bernard handing her his coffee-cup to be filled up. "That would always be your reaction to anything. Compassion. The virtue beyond all other virtues, that gives of itself so unstintingly that it drains its owner dry." He leaned forward to take the cup back and their eyes met and again there was that flash of intense awareness between them. "I'm doing a terrible thing to you, Rosalind," he went on with no trace of the usual mockery in his voice. "I'm adding another great burden to you who have already had more than enough to bear. I've no excuse except that I see in you this compassion that is fated to be exploited."

"Would you go on with your story, please," said Rosalind in a low voice. "Time's getting on, and I have to get a lunch for my son and his girl-friend."

"I'm sorry. I'll try to be brief now. Jane did her best to get Glenda out of the flat but she had a hopeless task because she had nothing to work on. It's easy enough to push a tottering marriage right over the edge and it is even possible, if you are skillful enough, to break up a reasonably harmonious partnership. Jane has no intellect but she is cunning and she has that sort of skill. If there had been any feeling of any sort left between Glenda and myself—not necessarily loving feeling, but bitterness, resentment, any sort of emotional bond—then Jane would have had a chance, but there was nothing between us except a sort of business partnership and the strong desire to keep that flat. Mutually advantageous business partnerships are much tougher nuts to crack than tolerably happy marriages."

"Yes, I suppose so," said Rosalind, feeling herself drawn into a discussion against her will and yet at the same time thinking how much she would enjoy his friendship and companionship if only it could remain at an impersonal level. "Yes, it's the financial and practical convenience of the marriage that's the hardest to break. Emotions are easy things to play with in comparison."

"Exactly." He beamed at her again. "Glenda and I had it all worked out to the last detail and we both smiled at Jane's attempts to create jealousy and discord. She did have a go at creating trouble for Glenda in her job, but Glen soon settled that. So the only thing left was for Glenda to have an accident. Too risky for anything to happen in the flat. Even if she got away with it as an accident, I should have known myself, and she'd have lost me—the object of the whole exercise. So she took a desperate gamble—another gambler, you see, Rosalind. She deliberately crashed that car."

"No, no. That's going too far," protested Rosalind. "She can't have done it intentionally."

"Accidental-done-on-purpose. Or a Freudian slip. Whichever you like to call it. That was it, Rosalind. She's confessed it to me since. Mind you, she was pretty well boozed up, for which I don't blame her, because it took more courage than anyone would have cold sober."

"But how did it happen? Why was Glenda travelling with you at all if you led separate lives?"

"Again a matter of convenience. One of the many advantages of our flat was the garage at the back of the block, which made it possible to run a car in Central London. But only one space per flat. Strict rationing. So we shared the car too. Perfectly amicably, just as we shared the flat. Jane liked driving, which I never did particularly, and chauffeuring me became part of her duties. Sometimes she drove us both if we had engagements in the same direction, as we did that day. Glenda was going to some sort of demo or protest rally—that was her life—and I was booked to lecture. Both in Hertfordshire. A foggy November evening. Normally on such occasions Glen sat in the back and I in front, but Jane said she wanted Glenda by her because she'd got better eyesight and was a better navigator in the fog. So there was Glen in the suicide seat and when we left the road and crashed into that tree it was Glen who was killed outright. She hadn't troubled to use her seat-belt. Jane had, and escaped fairly lightly. I was quite badly knocked about myself. I won't bore you with the details. The police and rescue services were stretched to the limit that night. Nobody worried about whether Jane had been drinking and nobody ever suggested that it was anything but an accident. There were similar smash-ups all along the motor-way. That's the way to murder somebody if you don't mind risking doing yourself in as well."

"I still don't believe it was deliberate," said Rosalind. "It was probably a sort of desperate carelessness. They do say that such road accidents are sometimes a form of concealed suicide, don't they?"

"They do," said Bernard. "But this wasn't suicide. However, if you want to give Jane the benefit of the doubt I won't try to stop you. I only want you to know my version of the story before she tells you that I leant over from the back seat and pulled the steering-wheel round at the fatal moment. That's what you are going to hear, and it's not true."

He got up from his chair and moved around the little living-room for a moment or two before coming to where Rosalind was sitting. There he crouched down in front of her so that his eyes were on a level with hers, and even at this moment of tension she noticed how very active and agile he was for a man of his age.

"It's not true, Rosalind," he repeated. "I did not cause that accident. Don't you believe me?"

"What I don't understand," said Rosalind, not avoiding his gaze but evading the question, "is why you married Jane after all this. I should have thought you would never want to see each other again."

"Yes, you would, wouldn't you?" Bernard laughed without amusement and straightened up again. "Well, if you don't believe I didn't crash that car, then you are certainly not going to believe me when I tell you why I married Jane. However."

He gave a slight shrug, an unhappy, uneasy gesture quite unlike his character as Rosalind thought she knew it.

"Here goes," he went on. "Jane was in a shocking state after the accident. Not so much physically, but mentally. She hadn't expected to be so ravaged by conscience. She told me she'd wanted Glenda to die but that now all she wanted was to kill herself. Whether she'd have done it or not I don't know, but she was certainly going through hell, and her drinking got more and more out of control. I felt so damned sorry for her that I married her. And now, my dear Rosalind, you may tell me that I am both a liar and a hypocrite and you want no more to do with me. If that's how you feel I shall quite understand, although I'll be very sorry about it. I'd wanted to be friends. I admire and respect you. I also like you. I wanted you to understand the sort of situation I am in but I wanted you to see it for yourself, without me spinning a long tale of misery first. But I've tried to be just a bit too clever as usual, and have made a thorough balls-up of the business. I'd better go now, as you'll be busy cooking for your youngsters. We'll forget the wager and I won't trouble you again. It was good of you to let me come this morning. Goodbye, Rosalind, and thank you for listening."

He held out his hand. Rosalind got to her feet but did not take the hand, and after a moment it fell back to his side.

"That was a very effective speech you have just made," said Rosalind surveying him appraisingly. "You know perfectly well that nobody who had any feeling in them at all could allow you to go away immediately after making such a speech. You have allowed yourself to show hurt and disappointment. You've thrown yourself on my charity and you've said you wanted me as a friend, which is a powerful appeal to someone in my position. Well done, Bernard."

He coloured faintly as he replied. "It wasn't intended to be like that. I've only spoken as I felt."

"Yes, that's the cleverness of it. When a normally reserved and calculating mind decides for once to come out into the open with the simple truth, it is irresistible."

He stared at her and then slowly shook his head. "You're

one up on me," he said. "Who's being too clever and subtle now?"

She laughed. "Let's stop fencing, shall we? You know perfectly well that I am not going to call you a liar and a hypocrite and that so far from not wanting any more to do with you, I want nothing more than to get to know you better. I don't know how much I believe of what you've told me about Jane. I'll have to see a bit more of both of you before I try to make up my mind."

"Even though I may be a murderer? You still want to be friends?"

She smiled but did not reply.

"For all you know, I caused that car to crash," he went on, "and for all you know, I may well be planning to poison Jane."

"For all you know, I aimed that hammer at my husband's head," retorted Rosalind, still smiling, "and for all you know I may be planning to poison Jane myself. Shall I tell you the truth now?"

"Yes, please."

"I like you, Bernard. On balance I don't think you are a murderer or a potential murderer, but I think you are a hard, vain, selfish, ambitious and possibly even cruel man. I also think you are easily hurt, very vulnerable at heart, very understanding and sympathetic to people in trouble, and capable of extraordinarily quixotic acts from time to time. Yes, I do believe you married Jane out of pity."

Bernard clutched his forehead and pretended to reel. "What a character! What a testimonial!" he cried.

"Isn't it true?"

"I don't know. I shall need several days of severe self-examination before I can come to an opinion. I'll let you know the result."

They moved towards the door of the living-room and there he added: "If you'd like to do the illustrations for me, Rosalind, the job's yours."

"But you don't know whether I'm any good," she protested. "Would you like to see a few of my things now?"

"Have you time?"

"About ten minutes."

She led the way through the kitchen into the tiny studio and opened up a portfolio of drawings and paintings. Bernard studied them without comment. Then she produced some table mats and book markers and other little items from drawers and laid them out for his inspection.

"There. Don't move them. That'll do for Deirdre to choose her present," she said. "Seen all you want?"

"Yes, thanks," he replied as they returned to the kitchen. "I like your style. Sufficiently accurate for the botanical information, but with a little imaginative touch about it too. It would be rather nice, I think, to have as colour plates paintings of flowers set in their natural habitat. Not a whole hedgerow or a copse, but the impression of it. Beatrix Potter style. Get me?"

"Yes, I'd like doing that," said Rosalind.

They talked about it for several minutes more, totally free from emotion or constraint of any kind, two people enthusiastically discussing a job on which they were to cooperate.

"You'd better come up and see my manuscript," said Bernard. "Tomorrow? No—weekends are probably awkward for you with your boy. Monday afternoon?"

They fixed the time and began to talk about the work again. The ten minutes that Rosalind had said she could spare were long over-run.

"There's going to be a special section on dangerous plants," said Bernard, "including things like foxgloves and laburnum and our old friend hemlock, with warnings about plants that could be mistaken for—"

"I know," interrupted Rosalind excitedly. "Let's put the pictures side by side—the safe plant and the poison one that looks like it. Let's take hemlock. Look." And she ran back into the studio and returned with a sheet of paper and a pencil and began to sketch, leaning over the kitchen table.

"There," she cried. "That would make a lovely page of illustrations. There's the killer in the oval panel in the middle and these plants round it are the harmless ones that look rather similar."

"Like a whodunit," said Bernard. "The guilty and the innocent gathered together to hear the verdict." He bent over the sketch with her and continued: "There's our *Conium maculatum*, and here we will have *Anthriscus sylvestris*—that's your cow parsley—and *Aethusa cynapium* and *Daucus carota* and—"

"Help!" cried Rosalind. "Don't you think we'd better put in the English names too?"

"Of course. All of them. Some plants have got dozens of popular names. Here on another page we'll have *Atropa belladonna*—"

"Deadly Nightshade?"

"Clever girl. That's right. And *Solanum dulcamara*—Woody Nightshade to you, madam—and other comparatively harmless berries. And we must give a prominent place to the other hemlock—the Hemlock Water Dropwort. He's a real stinker, is *Oenanthe crocata*, the king of our native killer-plants. I found some the other day by the stream that goes past the recreation ground. I'll mention it if I come to talk to your group again, because people ought to be alerted about it. There have been plenty of deaths both of humans and of cattle from this particular specimen. He's such a hypocrite, you see. His roots look like parsnips and his leaves look like celery and he doesn't even smell or taste bad. Rather pleasant, in fact, so I'm told. But eat him and you can be dead within the hour—horribly dead, with convulsions and madness sometimes coming first. I'll lend you some of the literature if you're interested."

"Thanks," said Rosalind. "I'll read the horror stories and perhaps they will inspire me to give him a suitably evil appearance. How about foxgloves?"

"They'll have to go in, of course, because digitalis is a poison, but I don't think anyone could really mistake any other plant for a foxglove. Then there's mistletoe berries."

"Ah, they're dangerous in more ways than one," said Rosalind, and they both laughed and did not hear the click of the gate.

—————— 5 ——————

Martin Bannister and Deirdre Parker heard the laughter as they crossed the small stone yard and came to the door at the side of the cottage. It was such happy, unaffected laughter that Deirdre, a curly, smiling and warm-hearted girl, began to laugh too, but she quickly stopped when she saw the frozen look on Martin's face.

"What's the matter?" she whispered.

"He's still here," replied Martin in a low and angry voice. "And he's got round her. I thought he was going to in spite of what she said."

"But, Martin—" Deirdre's round face looked very serious now—"she sounds so happy. I've never known your mother sound happy before. Surely you can't not want her to be happy?"

"Of course I want her to be happy," he snapped, "but this isn't the right way. He's only going to drag her into trouble. He's got rid of one wife and is trying to get rid of another."

"Ssh. We don't know that. It's all speculation. Your mother would never have made friends with him like this if she really believed he had done anything wrong."

"It's as I said. He's got round her."

"Oh Martin, please don't—"

Deirdre broke off. She knew what she wanted to say but the task of getting it across to Martin in his present mood was a very daunting one to her young mind, for she was always

43

uneasily conscious of the fact that as far as a happy home life went, she had had so much and Martin had had so little.

"Please don't what?" he said in the same tense and angry whisper.

"Please don't say anything. Not while Mr. Goodwin's still here, at any rate," concluded Deirdre lamely.

"Of course I won't say anything, as you put it. What d'you take me for? I don't make scenes in public, do I, in spite of my unfortunate parentage."

"Oh Martin!"

Deirdre looked up at the handsome boy who among her wide acquaintance was the first to have touched her heart and felt that heart full to overflowing with a mixture of love and pain and compassion.

"Let's go in," she said, not knowing how to endure the pressure of all these feelings and yet knowing that they were going to get worse and worse in the time to come.

She stretched out her hand towards the door, which in true village style was frequently left unlocked during the day, but before she could reach it the door was opened from within and they met, all four of them, the two older people standing closer together in the narrow passage, the two young ones in the little porch under the rambler roses. Rosalind and Bernard were in shadow, but Martin and Deirdre automatically stepped back slightly as the door opened and the morning sun lit up the boy's fair head and the girl's dark one.

"Hullo, my dears, you're just in time to meet a celebrity," said Rosalind.

It was said in the friendly but somehow impersonal manner that Swallowfields had come to know in her, and even at this moment it might have deceived Martin if he had not heard her earlier laughter, that happy and carefree laughter that had appealed to Deirdre but that Martin felt like stab wounds, all the worse because he knew civilized people should not feel this sort of primitive jealousy and rage.

Civilized man triumphed sufficiently for him to make suitably polite remarks when Rosalind introduced Bernard to them both. Nevertheless the underlying antagonism showed through, and Rosalind felt very grateful for Deirdre's warm and straightforward response.

"My mother is going to be green with envy when I tell her I've met you, Mr. Goodwin," she said. "She's got all your books and she's always lecturing Dad and me about our ignorance when we're looking round people's gardens. It's not that we don't like flowers and birds and things but you don't have time to do everything, do you, and music's my special thing, and Dad's so tired in the evenings when he gets back from the office that he just sits in front of the television set. He says working in Brighton nowadays is almost as bad as commuting to London."

"He's got a point there," said Bernard in his most charming manner. "I must say I'm very grateful not to have to commute anywhere. However, I'll have to go now and face the milling throng on the sea front since I'm supposed to be meeting someone for a late lunch."

"It's going to be very late," said Deirdre laughing. "The traffic's frightful."

"You two have got here very quickly, though," said Rosalind to Martin. "How did you manage it?"

"Deirdre drove us," he replied, not looking at his mother. "Mrs. Parker let her have the Mini for this morning."

"Where have you parked it?" asked Rosalind.

The tension in Martin was so strong that it was having an almost physical effect upon herself. Most of it arose from hostility to Bernard, but there was also an element of sore male pride that his girl-friend and not himself should have the use of the car. Rosalind saw and felt all this in Martin but had no means to comfort him. Bernard's earlier remark about talking of traffic problems in order to avoid emotional encounter returned vividly to her mind. What on earth did it matter where Deirdre had managed to squeeze in the Mini? What mattered was that she had let herself be swept away into a few minutes of thoughtless happiness, the joy that does not recognize itself because it consists of total absorption in something else, a total unawareness of self. She had never thought it would happen to her again, but it had happened while she was discussing the flower paintings with Bernard. There was a real meeting of minds on a creative enterprise, and he could have murdered ten wives and it would have made no difference. All that mattered was that she had known joy again.

Rosalind's mind took flight for a second or two into impossible heavens. When it returned to earth she discovered that in fact it did matter where Deirdre had parked the Mini after all.

"I'm awfully sorry," Bernard was saying, "but I'm afraid I'm going to have to ask you to shift it. I'll never be able to get past you in the entrance to the churchyard."

"Oh," said Deirdre in surprise, "is that old Renault yours? I thought it must be the vicar's. All right. I'm coming, Mr. Goodwin."

Goodbyes were said, and Bernard and Deirdre went off together to rearrange the cars, the girl chatting happily as she looked up at the older man walking by her side.

"He seems to have made yet another conquest," said Martin, looking after them.

Rosalind pulled him into the hall and shut the cottage door. Then she caught hold of him by the arms and spoke with great firmness.

"Now listen, Martin, you've got to snap out of this before you make both Deirdre and me miserable. We both love you so much that we deserve better treatment. I told you Bernard Goodwin was attractive to women. So are you. Long before you're his age you'll have collected dozens of admiring females. You're not doing so badly already. And as for your own poor old mother, well, I absolutely refuse to have you go and do a Hamlet act on me. I've no particular desire to marry again but I'm not going to cut myself off from all male company for ever, Martin, and you'll just have to accept it. I am not in love with Bernard Goodwin and in any case he's already got a wife, but I do like talking to him and I'm going to do the illustrations for his book."

Martin stiffened within her grasp but did not speak.

"Yes, we've arranged it and that was what we were talking about," went on Rosalind. "It's a real professional break-through for me and it also looks like being great fun. I'll be going to see them at Bell House on Monday afternoon and I'll make sure that I get a chance to talk to Jane Goodwin too and I shall do my best to help her. It's not going to be easy. The first wife was killed in a car crash and Bernard and Jane each accuse the other of being responsible. It's on the records as an accident on the motorway in a fog, with nobody to blame. That was the dramatic happening that has put them at each other's throats. I still don't know which one of them I believe, but I'm going to do my best not to take sides but to make the most of the opportunity for myself. Okay, so it probably is going to be very tense and fraught and no doubt I'll have to hear and see a lot that I'd rather not hear and see when I'm at their house. But at least I'll have a good solid job of work to do that will certainly lead to something more, and it'll be a damned sight more interesting than coffee mornings and Women's Institute meetings."

"Suppose people start gossiping?" said Martin in a low voice.

He had been listening with a very unhappy look on his face, but Rosalind felt sure she was doing the right thing in talking to him like this and in not taking refuge in any more pretence. It's going to have to come some time or other, she told herself. If it were the most suitable man in the world Martin would still take it badly. Even worse, in fact, because there might be a real danger in that case that she might marry again, whereas in the case of Bernard Goodwin there was no such danger.

"People will always gossip," she said aloud, "whether there's any foundation for it or not. If I get friendly with the Goodwins people in the village can hardly say worse things about me than no doubt they have said already. And I certainly shan't attempt to conceal anything because I've nothing to conceal. I'll telephone Lesley Green later today and tell her about the book illustrating. She'll be glad for my sake, and at least I shall know that it will be a friendly person who spreads the news around the village. And now I'd better go and get the lunch. I've put out some paintings for Deirdre to choose from for her present."

"Put them out for *him* to look at, you mean," said Martin.

Rosalind controlled herself with an effort and did not reply to this.

"I'll get the lunch," she repeated and went into the kitchen. A moment later the sound of footsteps on the stairs told her that Martin had gone up to his room and a little later there came the sound of a violin being tuned. Yes, we are right out of tune, thought Rosalind as she prepared the salad. There had never before, even during the worst of the times with Martin's father, been such painful tension between herself and her son. The cottage that up till now had been such a haven was full of the tension and it was only slightly eased when Deirdre's cheerful face came round the kitchen door and a voice asked, "Can I help?"

"Where's Martin?" she asked as she began to set the table.

"Upstairs," said Rosalind shortly.

"Oh." The girl's smile died away. "It's bad, then."

"Yes."

Into the ensuing silence came the sound of a few phrases being played on the violin.

"Haydn's *Creation*," said Deirdre. "Ouch! He's got that bit wrong. He always goes wrong there. So do we all, as a matter of fact."

"Deirdre," said Rosalind, standing opposite the girl at the other side of the kitchen table and holding a bowl of fruit in both hands. "Deirdre—please be kind to him. I can't—I can't—"

Her voice trembled and she bit her lips and put the bowl down on the table, feeling suddenly so giddy and faint that she could scarcely stand. A moment later she felt the warmth and strength of young arms encircling her and the girl's voice came as from a great distance.

"It's all right, Mrs. Bannister. It's all right, Rosalind. Truly it is."

"I'm sorry," muttered Rosalind. "I didn't mean—"

And then the fountain overflowed and all the strain of years and the mental and emotional turmoil of the last days came out in a burst of weeping, while the difficult phrase was repeated again and again on the violin in the room above.

"He's actually got it right at last," said Deirdre. "Are you feeling better now, Mrs. Bannister?"

Rosalind nodded, wiping her face and smoothing down her hair.

"Mr. Goodwin says you're going to do the pictures for his new book," said the girl. "I think that's super. It'll really get you known, won't it?"

"I hope so," said Rosalind. "But Martin doesn't."

"I'll deal with Martin," said Deirdre with far more confidence than she really felt. "You get on with your own life. It's time something nice happened for you."

"I don't think he'd actually mind my doing the work," said Rosalind, "if it were for anybody else but Bernard Goodwin. Perhaps I ought to have pretended to Martin that I had no interest in him as a person at all, only as a working colleague. Perhaps I shouldn't have told Martin about Bernard's wife and all the misery in that household. But I'm so sick of pretending and Martin's got to face it one day . . . and it seemed better to get the row over straight away instead of having it rumbling in the background for ages before it blew up . . . What do you think, Deirdre? Ought I to have told Martin anything? Or should I have pretended to him that I had no interest in anybody or anything? Or perhaps I'd better tell Bernard that I can't do the work after all and try to keep away from the Goodwins entirely."

"No," said Deirdre firmly. "That's the one thing you mustn't do. You've got to go on with your own career. Suppose you were a man who'd been given the chance of a big step forward. You'd never dream of turning it down, would you, however many personal complications it might lead you into. Of course you wouldn't. Careers come first."

"Thanks, Deirdre," said Rosalind with a faint smile.

"And I don't quite see how you could have prevented Martin from knowing that you enjoy talking to Mr. Goodwin," continued the girl. "However much you tried to pretend, he'd still have got jealous. He heard you laughing before we came in just now. I thought it was lovely but of course he didn't like it. No, you were quite right to tell him that straight out. The only thing I'm doubtful about is whether you ought to have told him this business about Mr. Goodwin's wife saying he's planning to murder her. I'm sure it will turn out to be all imagination, but the trouble is that it gives Martin such a hold over you all, if you see what I mean."

"Yes, I do see," said Rosalind, no longer smiling.

"It's not that there's any danger of Martin spreading stories about Mr. Goodwin around the village," continued Deirdre very thoughtfully. "He told me about it, of course, but that's different, and I've said nothing to anybody else so far. If I ever tell anyone, it will be Dad, and he's used to keeping people's secrets. In fact it was he who told me that you can't be too careful about possible slander, quite apart from not hurting people. I know Martin agrees with me on that. But he could use it against you, and he wouldn't think that wrong because he'd believe he was doing it for your own good. He could keep reminding you about it in all sorts of ways and make your working with Mr. Goodwin even more awkward than it might be in any case, with this problem of his wife. Why did you have to tell Martin about these suspicions? I know you two are very close friends and not like different generations at all, and of course he's very sensible about most things and gives good advice, but when it's a case of him being very emotionally involved himself—"

"Oh, I know, I know!" interrupted Rosalind. "I can see now that I ought not to have told him. It was my cowardice. I knew Martin was going to be jealous of Bernard whatever happened and I suppose I thought I could somehow buy his goodwill by treating him as an equal and pretending to ask his advice. It wasn't only cowardly. It was stupid too. But I've done it and it's too late to go back. So what am I to do now, Deirdre?"

And the woman who was so used to carrying her own burdens and those of others looked helplessly at the young girl who was so happily alive and blessed by all the good things of life.

"Since you can't undo it," said Deirdre, obviously thinking very hard, "I think the only thing is to go on as you began and keep Martin right in the picture. I mean, he wasn't actually openly rude to Mr. Goodwin just now, so there's no reason why they shouldn't go on meeting each other. Why don't you take him along too when you go up to Bell House? Then he can meet Mrs. Goodwin as well as see the set-up for himself, and if there is really anything that looks suspicious then you can talk about it together. If Martin is right in the middle of it with you he's going to feel less jealous. I'm quite sure of that."

"I think you're right," said Rosalind, impressed by Deirdre's voice and manner. "I believe you know Martin better than I do."

Deirdre looked pleased. "I'll go and fetch him," she said. "He'll have practised himself into a better mood by now."

She ran upstairs and was gone for some time, while Rosalind thought over what Deirdre had said about bringing Martin and the Goodwins together. It had sounded a good idea in the girl's bright confident presence, but looking at it more coolly she could see that it was full of dangers, and she had more or less decided, when the two young people came into the kitchen at last, that whatever the awkwardness and strain between Martin and herself, it would be better in the long run to keep him away from Bernard and Jane.

"What's to eat?" asked Martin, sitting down at the table. "Cheese flan, cold turkey . . . Deirdre and I are practically starving. We've had nothing to eat since the swim and we've raised eighty pounds for the new sports ground."

"Well done," said Rosalind. It was obvious that Martin was making a very determined effort to be his usual self. Deirdre must have been lecturing him to good effect. For a moment Rosalind enjoyed the delightful sensation that everything was going to be all right, and then Deirdre spoke and her apprehension returned in full force.

"Martin's longing to meet Mrs. Goodwin," she said, "and to see the set-up at Bell House for himself. There's nothing on at school on Monday afternoon and he was wondering whether he could come along with you."

"Do you really want to come?" Rosalind asked Martin.

"Yes, definitely," he replied with his mouth full. "I can keep an eye on you in the magician's kitchen and have a peep at whatever is boiling up in the witches' cauldron. And no doubt we shall get a long lecture on plants, which will do me good. You're always telling me how ignorant I am in that respect, aren't you, Mum?"

It was said in a light-hearted and jokey manner and it looked on the face of it as if Deirdre had managed to restore Martin to his usual balance. The next few hours passed pleasantly enough. Deirdre selected a little water-colour sketch of the cottage from among Rosalind's paintings and then they all lay in the back garden and sunbathed. What the young people were thinking about, if indeed they were thinking at all, Rosalind did not know, but for her this lazy Saturday afternoon was heavy with foreboding, despite the appearance of harmony.

6

When Rosalind telephoned Bell House to ask whether she might bring Martin with her, Jane Goodwin answered the phone and was very gushing.

"I'd love to meet your son," she said. "I hardly see anybody from one week's end to the next and it'll be a great treat to meet a nice-looking boy. I'm sure he's a nice-looking boy, isn't he?"

She gave a little giggle that made Rosalind wonder whether she was slightly drunk. John Bannister, during the last years of his life, had always been a lot more than slightly drunk by eleven o'clock on a Sunday morning. Sundays had been the worst of all.

"I expect you'll like Martin," she said. "He's studying science mainly but he loves music and plays the violin a bit."

"How dreamy!" cried Jane. "I simply can't wait."

"Is Bernard available at the moment?" asked Rosalind, feeling that she could not take very much more of this sort of thing in her present state of mind.

Jane laughed, and the fact that she had been drinking became even more evident. "On Sunday morning? You must be joking. He's gone to church. I told you. He's gone to try and save his soul. As if he'd got a hope!"

"Yes, you told me. I'd forgotten," said Rosalind. "Would you tell him that Martin will be coming with me tomorrow afternoon?"

"A tea-party! We'll have a tea-party," cried Jane. "Won't that be fun?"

Rosalind said she would look forward to it and rang off. The heavy sense of foreboding turned into an absolute certainty of disaster. It was obvious what Jane's behaviour to Martin was going to be like. His own attitude to her would probably depend upon whether or not she had been drinking heavily when they arrived on the morrow. If she had, it would put Martin off at once. He had seen enough of alcoholism never to want to encounter it again, and one of the many attractions that Deirdre held for him was that she drank very little. But if Jane had not been drinking, or had managed successfully to conceal the fact that she had, and was just nervous as she had been at the Women's Institute meeting, it would be quite a different story. All Martin's protective and chivalrous instincts would be aroused, and since he was determined to see in Jane a victim and in Bernard a villain, and since Jane was very handsome, and no doubt would take special pains for Martin's sake, and for a boy of Martin's age a beautiful woman considerably older than himself had a special appeal . . .

Rosalind's thoughts raced on, and she found herself worrying so much that she was very tempted to call the whole thing off completely. If only she could get hold of Bernard by himself and tell him, she felt sure that he would understand her reasons and not try to persuade her. Whatever pleasure she found in his company, and whatever the professional and financial advantages to herself, it was not worth it to have this agony of apprehension about Martin.

How to get Bernard alone was the problem. For one wild moment she even thought of standing in the entrance to the churchyard and catching him as he came out of the morning service. Then she scolded herself and told herself that she was losing her judgement completely. There was always a sizeable congregation for this service, including many members of the Women's Institute and their families, and for Rosalind to make her way through the little groups of chatting people and go up to Bernard and talk to him was the surest way of calling the whole village's attention to them both.

Unless she found where he had parked the car and pretended

she had just happened to be walking past . . . But he had probably walked in to Swallowfields. It was only fifteen or twenty minutes' walk from Bell House and she knew he liked walking and disliked driving.

Rosalind gave it up and concentrated instead on the business of keeping up an appearance of cheerful normality with Martin, which was not too difficult for most of the day, because he seemed to be determined to do the same. It was not until late on the Sunday evening that there came another little foretaste of what was to come. They had listened to a few records together and then, by mutual consent, each picked up a book and there was silence in the little living-room for some time. At about ten o'clock Martin said he would fetch some tea and biscuits, which was also part of the normal programme when they were at home together for the evening, and after he had gone out of the room Rosalind gave way to her desire to find out what he had been reading. Normally she was scrupulously careful about Martin's privacy and would always wait for him to tell her what he was reading or writing or thinking, and never ask him anything unless she was quite certain that he wanted to be asked.

She put down the book on British wild flowers that she had been studying with some care, having decided that whatever happened at Jane's tea-party in the way of emotional upsets, she herself had a job to do at Bell House and she must be able to talk intelligently to Bernard about plants.

Martin's book was a much less weighty tome than her own. It was a little dark blue volume in a pocket classics series, in good condition but slightly faded down the spine. He had left it open face downwards, in the chair on which he had been sitting. Rosalind picked it up, turned it over, and read to herself:

> Apollodorus . . . burst into a loud cry, and made us one and all break down by his sobbing and grief, except only Socrates himself. "What are you doing, my friends?" he exclaimed. "I sent away the women chiefly in order that they might not offend in this way, for I have heard that a man should die in

silence. So calm yourself and bear up." When we heard that we were ashamed, and we ceased from weeping. But he walked about, until he said that his legs were getting heavy, and then he lay down on his back as he was told. And the man who gave the poison began to examine his feet and legs from time to time: then he pressed his foot hard, and asked if there was any feeling in it; and Socrates said, No: and then his legs, and so higher and higher, and showed us that he was cold and stiff. And Socrates felt himself, and said when it came to his heart, he should be gone.

Rosalind stopped reading and looked inside the front cover of the book. There on the fly leaf was written in her own small neat hand: "Rosalind Frances Burton. Sixth Form, St. Joseph's School, London NW3."

She stood staring at the writing on the yellowing page and the little sitting-room in the cottage in Swallowfields faded away and Martin and his father John alike were wiped out in the backward roll of time. She was Rosalind Frances Burton, clever and idealistic, a school prefect and popular with staff and with pupils of all ages; planning to go to art college after leaving school, but very interested in many other things, including music and philosophy.

The Trial and Death of Socrates. How she had loved the book and sought strength from it again and again after her teenage revolt against her own religious upbringing, a very emotional revolt that had distressed her father, tolerant clergyman though he had been. If he were alive now he would be hard put to it not to tell her she had brought her troubles upon herself by her impulsiveness.

Rosalind held the little book tenderly in both hands and memory surged over her like a great flood of light, dimming all present time and place and feeling, so that when a voice spoke she barely heard it and when she became conscious that another human being was near her she was momentarily unable to recognize who it was.

Martin put the tray he was carrying down on the coffee table, rushed forward and snatched the book from his mother's hand, and began to rage.

"For Christ's sake, can't I even read what I like without you spying on me?"

Rosalind stood in silent bewilderment, caught in a mental no-man's-land between past and present, her fingers gently curved round as if she were still holding the book in her hands.

"You're always complaining that I'm too narrowly scientific," continued Martin in the same furious tones. "You ought to be pleased to find me reading *The Trial and Death of Socrates*."

Rosalind's hands fell to her sides at last and she took a deep breath.

"I'm sorry, darling," she said, "I didn't mean to pry. I recognized my old school copy, that's all, and it brought back so many memories that for the moment I didn't know where I was."

He glared at her and moved across to pick up the book on wild flowers she had been studying.

"Meadow saffron," he read aloud. "Flowers light purple or white like a crocus. Leaves and fruit contain an alkaline substance of a very poisonous nature called colchicine. Grows wild in meadows." He glanced up at her. "So that's to be the one, is it?" he said. "Not hemlock, but poisonous wild crocus. Presumably it is just as effective. I suppose the idea is to extract some of the juice and feed it to his wife. But how is he going to disguise the taste? And does he propose to plead that he didn't know it was poisonous or that he made a mistake and thought it was a different plant?"

Martin began to laugh, almost as hysterically as Jane Goodwin had laughed. Rosalind had not known him like this since the hour of his father's death, when he had reacted with just this wild uncontrolled laughter.

"No good his pleading ignorance," he cried. "You or I might get away with it but not the well-known botanical expert."

"Stop that at once!" shouted Rosalind. "Have you gone out of your mind?"

The sounds gradually subsided and Rosalind sat down again,

suddenly feeling too weak to stand, and shut her eyes. When she opened them a little later she saw that Martin had brought her a cup of tea and was holding it out to her. She thanked him and took it.

"I'm sorry," he said in a very subdued voice. "It's a long time since I've been like that, isn't it?"

Rosalind came to a resolution.

"Now listen," she said very firmly. "This is what we are going to do. Or rather not do. We are not going to Bell House tomorrow and I am going to have nothing more to do with Jane and Bernard Goodwin. And I am not going to do that illustrating job. It's too late to get a letter in the post and I don't want to telephone, but I will write a very brief note explaining why we aren't coming—you shall help me draft it—and I'll ask Lesley if she'll drive up there tomorrow morning and drop it in by hand. I won't pretend I'm not disappointed about the job, but it is not worth it—nothing is worth it—if it's going to do this to you."

She paused and looked at Martin. He continued to stare at the floor and say nothing.

"I also think the time has come for us to leave Swallowfields," continued Rosalind. "I've been thinking about it for some time and this has decided me. If you're going to Exeter to university I might as well move to the West Country too. I'll find another cottage and you can come home at weekends if you like, and we'll start again and forget all this. That's what I've decided, Martin, and I know it's for the best. If Deirdre gets her place at Exeter too, that will be fine. If not, then you and she will have to arrange to meet as best you can. You'll both always be welcome at my cottage."

"I'm not worried about Deirdre," said Martin. "I'm only thinking about you. You've really fallen for Bernard Goodwin, haven't you?"

"I told you I'm very attracted to him," said Rosalind stiffly.

"Oh, for God's sake don't prevaricate!" cried Martin, showing signs of becoming agitated again. "Can't we have the truth for once? You've fallen in love with him."

"All right then. Yes."

"But he's got a wife so you must wish that wife were out of the way and leave the field clear for you."

"That doesn't necessarily follow," said Rosalind.

"Of course it follows. You're kidding yourself if you think it doesn't. You'd like Jane Goodwin dead. Or divorced."

"No!" cried Rosalind. "I don't wish Jane or anybody else dead. It's much too early to say what I'd like to happen. My feelings are much too confused. At the moment I would just like some peace."

"Then there's the question of this job," went on Martin stubbornly. "It's a wonderful chance for you and you may never get one like it again. If you give it up because of me you're going to feel resentful towards me for ever after and neither of us could stand that."

"I should try not to," said Rosalind.

"Yes, but you wouldn't succeed. You're not one of those self-sacrificing mothers. We've got to look at this straight. This is how I see it. If we do what you've just suggested then you're going to lose the job and the man and your home and the life in the village here, which I know you like, or at any rate you've got used to. If you stay here you've got work that you'll do well and that will probably lead on to something else and you've still got your home and your acquaintances. That's the credit side. I'm not putting Bernard Goodwin on the credit side because although you feel like that about him I know he is going to bring you misery and nothing else. If he doesn't feel the same way about you, you'll be miserable. And if he does feel the same way, you'll be even more miserable because you'll be terrified that he is going to get rid of his wife. There's no joy there for you either way. Is there?"

Rosalind looked across at him. He was sitting leaning forward with his hands dropping between his knees. His face was flushed and deadly serious. He had with an enormous effort of self-control put his own feelings aside to try to look at the position in a detached and practical way. She admired him for it and pitied him and loved him too, but the last thing she wanted at this moment was a cool, clear-headed look at her own situation. She was in the sort of emotional turmoil that cannot endure the sharp outlines and sharp clarity of truth, but that needs the protection of illusion and false hope and self-deception in order that the mind can stabilize itself and renew its strength. But Martin was too young to understand this, and at the moment she had not the strength to try to explain it to him.

"Of course you're right, darling," she murmured. "But I don't think I can discuss it any more tonight. I'm much too tired."

"All right," said Martin, "but you're not to cancel tomorrow or I'll never forgive you. We can't get out of it that way."

Rosalind lifted her hand and then let it fall again in a gesture of total helplessness.

"I want to meet Jane Goodwin," said Martin. "I want to see them both at home together so I can make up my own mind. Maybe after I've met her I won't think so badly of him after all. Or maybe I'll think even worse. But I want to see for myself so that I can judge for both of us. You see, Mum—," and he came and put a protective arm round her—"you're a little bewitched at the moment and you're not seeing clearly at all. But one of us has got to try to see clearly if you're to be saved from getting into a frightful mess. You can't afford to get into any more messes. Not after what happened to Dad."

"No," agreed Rosalind, not knowing whether she felt more like laughing or weeping, "I certainly can't afford to get into any more messes, and at least one of us must try to keep a balanced and unbiased view."

7

Bell House was about fifteen minutes' walk from the heart of Swallowfields, along a lane that wound gently up the slope of the Downs. The house had a better view than most of its neighbours but the building itself was substantial and comfortable-looking rather than interesting or picturesque.

"Must cost something to keep up this place," said Martin as they walked along the drive.

"He has private means, I believe," said Rosalind. "Free-lancing is a chancy business even when you seem to be riding on the crest of a wave."

"As we know only too well from Dad's misfortunes," said Martin.

This was the fourth or fifth time that day that Martin had spoken to Rosalind of his father. Since normally they rarely mentioned John Bannister, this was most noticeable. It might, of course, simply be due to Martin's overwrought state of mind, but Rosalind was more inclined to think that he was doing it deliberately as a sort of warning or even a threat to her. Don't think you are free to do as you like, he seemed to be saying: remember you are a woman with a past, and anything you do now is going to have to be built on that past. He hates Bernard, she said to herself: does he think that by throwing us together he will be taking the quickest way to get Bernard out of my life?

Before yesterday evening Rosalind would have challenged

Martin with this straight out. But yesterday evening had changed things between the two of them. In spite of Martin's temporary collapse into hysteria, he had somehow or other emerged the victor. Rosalind had up till now taken all the important decisions about their life, after considering Martin's views, but this time the decision was Martin's and his alone. She had been firmly resolved not to come to Bell House and to put both Bernard and Swallowfields behind her as quickly as possible. That they were now standing at the front door of Bernard's house waiting for somebody to answer their ring was entirely due to Martin. She believed she knew his motives and she believed him to be utterly wrong in his decision, but she no longer had any control over him.

Not only no control: it was worse than that. Rosalind was actually beginning to be afraid of her son.

They stood silently together until the door was opened and then for a brief moment they were united by a common surprise. For it was neither Bernard nor Jane who stood there, but a boy of about Martin's age or a little older, a very ordinary-looking sort of boy, neither tall nor short, dark nor fair. The only thing that was unusual about him was the broad smile on his face. It was not simply a faint smile of welcome, but a fixed smile that did not vary and that was rather uncanny because there was no laughter in his eyes. These were dark and unhappy-looking, like a lost dog's.

A nephew or other relative? A friend? A plumber or some other tradesman? Or a protégé of some sort?

The thoughts flashed in quick succession through Rosalind's mind and she knew that the same process was going on in Martin's. The only thing the young man could not be was a son, because the Goodwins had no child.

Rosalind recovered first from the surprise.

"Are Mr. and Mrs. Goodwin in?" she asked.

The boy made no reply but simply inclined his head slightly, the set smile remaining in place, and opened the door wide for them to pass through.

"Thank you," said Rosalind, feeling more and more puzzled.

The large hall smelt pleasantly of lavender but it was rather too dark for her liking. Even on this sunny day, and with several doors leading off from it and left open, the dark oak furnishings were oppressive and she was glad when Bernard appeared in one of the doorways and took them into a big room with two large bay windows and a much more cheerful air.

"This is Garry," he said to Rosalind and Martin. "Our indispensable Garry."

Rosalind smiled at the boy and Martin said, "Hullo" in an awkward way, and then there was a silence, while Garry's smile did not waver but neither did he make a sound.

"Would you go and tell Jane they're here?" said Bernard. "She's in the summer-house, I think, and she wouldn't have heard the bell."

The boy left the room, rather to Rosalind's relief, for she was beginning to find the smile and the silence distressing.

"He's a mute," said Bernard, after waiting for a moment for Garry to get out of hearing. "Not a deaf-mute. His hearing is perfectly normal but he has practically no speech."

"How do you communicate with him?" asked Rosalind.

Martin had walked over to one of the windows and was looking at the view, and she knew that he was suffering from the mixture of revulsion and guilt that so often accompanies an encounter with severe physical disability. It had even taken the sting out of the meeting with Bernard. Had Bernard, knowing Martin's dislike and distrust of himself, planned it this way? Rosalind could not help feeling that it was not by chance that the disconcertingly speechless Garry had opened the door to them.

"That's not the problem," said Bernard with his most pleasant and easy smile. "It's how does he communicate with us that you ought to be asking. Actually he is able to make some sounds—not very charming to listen to, and he never attempts them in front of strangers because he is very self-conscious. However, it is sometimes possible to interpret them, and Jane is better at it than I am."

This surprised Rosalind. She would not have expected, from what she had seen and heard of Jane, that she would have had either the patience or the steadiness of nerve to learn to make sense of a dumb boy's attempts at speech. Bernard's next remark partly explained the mystery.

"Garry will do anything for Jane," he said. "He helps in the house and the garden and he's quite a help to me as well. He is intelligent and very conscientious and seems to be genuinely interested in learning how to deal with herbs."

"The sorcerer's apprentice," said Martin, turning round from the window and glancing first at Bernard and then at his mother.

"That's right," said Bernard, as amiably as if he had never heard this joke before, although Rosalind felt sure he must have heard it many times. "He helps stir the witches' cauldron. Incidentally," he continued in the same friendly tone of voice, "I am not in any sense whatever qualified to call myself a herbalist. There is a long and rigorous training required in order to practise in herbal medicine and rigid rules governing the practice. All I am is a journalist, on a par with any other scientific or technical journalist, but I'm luckier than most because I've got the time and money and opportunity to dabble a little myself in addition to studying the experts and trying to make them more intelligible to a lay audience. And the subject of herbal medicine is an easy one for the amateur or the journalist to dabble in himself, which makes for misunderstanding. Unlike heart surgery, for example. Nobody would expect a television interviewer doing a series of modern surgery actually to have wielded the scalpel himself. But picking and drying cowslip flowers and brewing cowslip tea—which incidentally will send you to sleep as well as any barbiturate—is a different matter altogether as far as the viewers and readers are concerned."

"Anyone can do it," said Rosalind.

"Exactly. And anyone can do a lot of other things that can result in a product less innocent than cowslip tea."

"And anyone can go to the chemist and dose themselves with something that is quite unsuited to their condition," returned Rosalind. "Neither you nor anybody else can prevent people from trying to diagnose their own ailments and treating themselves. I'm quite sure the manufacturers of patent medicines haven't got any scruples about the abuse of their products so long as their profits look healthy."

"Possibly not, but then they are faceless men. No one can get at them. But I have a face and a voice that is known to quite a number of people, and if I pass on some knowledge that I have learned from the experts and somebody makes a bad use of it, there are plenty of people who will hold me responsible for the unfortunate result. This is why I like to try things out for myself as far as possible before I write about them. If I am passing on a receipt that has been given me I make it up myself and I even dose myself with it. That's the only way to find the snags. Do it yourself. But I never, repeat never, hand over any homemade remedy to another individual. Not even to a close friend. Not even to a member of my own household. I pass on information and I tell people what difficulties I myself have experienced in my experiments. That is all."

"It's never a good idea to hand on any sort of medicine to anyone else," said Rosalind. "I think you are very wise to refrain from doing so."

"If it's true that he does refrain. Personally I doubt it."

Martin said this in a very low voice and then turned back to look out of the window again. Behind his back Rosalind and Bernard glanced at each other. Rosalind's look signalled apology and appeal: Bernard's replied with tolerance and understanding.

"If you'd like to come and have a look at my working shed after tea," said Bernard in the same courteous manner, "I'd be delighted to show you round. I don't do any experimenting in the house, because the brewing and sometimes even the drying of plants can sometimes be a rather smelly business, especially when it goes wrong. And the kitchen part of the shed is well insulated from the study part where I do my writing and thinking."

"I'd like to see it very much," said Rosalind. She glanced towards Martin, who was still standing with his back to them. The hostility and suspicion that emanated from that back filled the room. Bernard's little explanatory speech had done nothing to dispel it. In fact if anything it had made matters worse. Rosalind could read Martin's mind and knew that the boy felt as if Bernard's lecture had been directed at him. As indeed it had, thought Rosalind, and quite rightly so, but also quite uselessly, because it was obvious that Martin was determined to disbelieve anything Bernard might say.

Rosalind began to long for Jane and the dumb boy, Garry, to appear. Their arrival would no doubt bring a whole host of fresh embarrassments, but at least it would put an end to the present tension and awkwardness between the three of them.

"We'll go round after tea, then," said Bernard, "and I'll show you my notes to date and the specimens that I should like paintings made of. If Martin cares to come too he will be very welcome, but if it would not interest him, then perhaps he would be kind enough to stay and entertain Jane for a while. She gets very bored with people being shown the shed and would be grateful for some agreeable company."

It would not be easy, thought Rosalind, for Martin to think up a really offensive reply to this tactful speech, but she was not to learn whether or not Martin would have succeeded, because as Bernard finished speaking Jane made her entrance. It really was an entrance, so determinedly dramatic that it was impossible not to respond in like manner, and for a second or two Rosalind saw them all, the whole four of them, as if they were characters on a stage set, playing to an audience, speaking and acting as they had been told to and with no wills of their own.

"Rosalind!" cried Jane, as if they were the closest of friends. "How lovely to see you! And Martin. You can't think how much I've been looking forward to meeting you." And she held out a hand to each, her right to Rosalind and her left to Martin, and smiled at each of them in turn.

"It's nice to see you too," said Rosalind, "and I'm glad you're looking better than last time we met."

She had not meant to say this. It was hardly tactful to remind Jane of the scene outside the village hall, but the devil who seemed to be pulling the strings and writing the play put the words into her mouth. She's jealous, the audience would think; jealous of this gorgeous woman who is so much more handsome than she is and younger too, and who has such a charming husband and a lovely house. They might be right too, thought Rosalind as she disengaged her hand from Jane's. I believe I am jealous. At any rate I've never felt quite like this before. I really hate her and I can't find any pity in me for her at all.

At the moment, however, Jane Goodwin did not appear to be in any particular need of pity. She did not look at all nervous. She was glowing and welcoming and very lovely, and she was obviously making a great impression upon Martin. Rosalind suspected that she had been drinking pretty heavily in order to gain the poise and the confidence to put on the act, but there was as yet no outward sign of it. It was plain that the whole scene was primarily directed at Martin, and he was obligingly playing the part allotted to him.

"Your mother tells me you are a violinist," said Jane. "I envy you. It must be a great source of joy."

"I'm not much good," replied Martin, "but we certainly enjoy ourselves."

"To have something that you really love doing," said Jane, suddenly looking serious and a trifle wistful, "even if you don't do it very well, but that brings you together with people who share your enthusiasm . . ."

She had hit exactly the right note for Martin. Friendliness towards his mother and a lively interest in himself that had every appearance of sincerity, combined with her apparently quite unself-conscious beauty to win him over completely. They sat near to each other by one of the bay windows and Bernard and Rosalind took armchairs facing the other window.

"I've been thinking over our talk the other day," said Bernard to Rosalind, "and have drafted out a scheme for the illustrations of the poisonous plants."

Rosalind tried to make a suitable response but her mind was only half on the subject, much as she was looking forward to doing the work. Out of the corner of her eye she could see Martin and Jane talking animatedly, and she could not help wondering what Bernard was thinking about it. He seemed to be taking no notice of the others at all, and Rosalind found it impossible to tell what he thought of Jane's behaviour.

"Don't you think that's the best way to get round that problem?" said Bernard's voice.

"I'm sorry," said Rosalind. "I'm afraid I wasn't listening properly. I thought perhaps we would not be talking business until after tea. I really am sorry. I'll try to concentrate more now."

"It's all right. I understand," he said, and the next moment the door opened and Garry came in with the tea trolley and Rosalind witnessed a new development in the drama.

When the mute boy first came into the room his eyes were looking down at the trolley that he was guiding and there was the same set smile on his face. This faded when he looked up and saw Jane smiling at Martin and listening intently to what he was saying and not even turning her head when Garry entered the room. Garry's face without the smile looked quite different, and Rosalind noticed for the first time how extremely expressive were the dark eyes. The commonplace phrase so lightly used, "If looks could kill," came into her mind. The eyes of the dumb boy looked as if they would gladly kill; they expressed all the meaning that the tongue was unable to utter as he wheeled the trolley into a position for Jane to pour the tea.

She turned at last and smiled up at him, the same beaming smile that she had been directing at Martin, but the mute boy did not melt, and Rosalind wondered whether Martin recognized the passion of jealousy in the dark eyes or whether he was so blinded by Jane's attentions that he could see nothing else.

The drama in dumb show came to an end at last.

"Thanks, Garry," said Jane. "I think that's everything we need. It looks a lovely tea. Thank you very much. I hope you have kept some of those delicious-looking sandwiches for yourself."

So he is not to eat with us, thought Rosalind; not when there is company present. In one way she felt this as a relief, but at the same time she was torn with pity for the boy, dismissed from the scene after he had witnessed Jane bestowing her favours on another.

"Does he have meals with you when you are on your own?" she asked Jane after Garry had left the room.

"Oh dear, the ambiguities of the English language!" cried Jane with a glance at Martin. "Do you mean when Bernard and

I are together or when Bernard is out and there is only myself?"

"Both," said Rosalind, trying hard not to sound abrupt but feeling more and more irritated with Jane every moment.

"Then the answers are not the same," said Jane. "Garry and I eat together when I'm by myself. It would be rather absurd, wouldn't it, for me to sit in solitary state at the dining-room table and for Garry to sit alone in the kitchen. But when Bernard is at home for a meal—" and Jane made this sound as if it were a rare occurrence—"he doesn't like having Garry eat with us because he finds it embarrassing. As if the boy could help the noises he makes, poor thing."

Rosalind began to wish that she had never raised the subject at all. She glanced at Bernard who said nothing, but Rosalind believed she could see distress as well as repressed fury in his face and she felt an overwhelming desire to defend him against Jane's attacks.

"Perhaps Garry prefers to have his meals alone," she said. "It must be less effort for him. I think I'd probably prefer it in his case."

"I wouldn't," cried Martin, rounding on his mother. "I'd loathe to be shut away as if I were something to be ashamed of."

"I didn't say that," said Rosalind.

"You meant it, though," retorted Martin. "It's sheer hypocrisy—this pretending that keeping disabled people out of sight is for their own good."

"I quite agree with you," said Rosalind. "We've discussed this matter before. But there's no question of being kept out of sight in this case. Garry opened the door to us."

"Then why isn't he having tea with us now?"

Rosalind looked at Bernard and then at Jane. "What frightful visitors you must think us," she said trying to speak lightly and make a joke of it. "You very kindly invite Martin and me to tea and to see your house and garden and all we do is make rude remarks and argue about how you ought to behave in your own household!"

"Don't mind me," said Jane very sweetly. "We love having people who feel they can behave naturally. Don't we, Bernie?"

Bernard took a bite from a slice of cake and made no reply.

"After all," continued Jane, "we always behave perfectly naturally ourselves in front of visitors."

"Do you?" said Rosalind, suddenly deciding that the whole situation was now so hopeless that she might as well throw all caution away and say exactly what she was thinking. "I should have thought your own present behaviour was very unnatural. You are obviously trying to give a false impression of yourself to Martin and to show Bernard up badly."

"Mother! I think you ought to apologize for that at once!" cried Martin, getting to his feet to emphasize his indignation.

"Don't be angry with her, Martin," said Jane in a voice that sounded very close to tears. "It's quite true that I have been making a special effort to make this a pleasant occasion for you and that normally I don't have much in my life to be cheerful and happy about. I suffer from a kind of illness that doesn't show any outward symptoms but that is very hard to cure. Your mother knows all about it, and it's because she was so understanding and sympathetic when I met her last week that I find it so hard that she should say to me now . . ."

The voice faded away most effectively. Martin continued to glare at Rosalind. Bernard drained his cup and got to his feet.

"This seems to be the right moment," he said, "for Rosalind and me to retire and get down to work, since Jane has suitably prepared the ground for telling Martin all about how I killed my first wife and how I am now planning to do away with herself. It's a most intriguing story, Martin. You are going to be held spellbound. Do you want me to send Garry in to clear away, Jane? I don't know whether you'd like to make your peace with him now or whether you'd rather torment him a bit more first."

To this speech Jane not surprisingly made no response except to burst into tears.

"All right," said Bernard. "I take it that you don't want Garry brought in again just yet. Rosalind and I will go, then. Try not to overdo it with Martin. You've been perfect up till now, but when you get too carried away you sometimes overdo things. Come, Rosalind."

He held open the door for her and Rosalind left the room with the impression of Martin's look of outrage firmly printed on her mind.

Garry was in the hall. The smile returned to his face as they emerged but it was impossible to tell whether he had overheard any of their talk.

"We're going to the shed," said Bernard, "and I'm going to give Mrs. Bannister those specimens to paint. You've put them in the fridge, all labelled ready for her, haven't you, Garry?"

The boy nodded vigorously.

"Thanks," said Bernard. "I don't think the others have finished tea yet," he added as Garry made a movement towards the sitting-room door, "but Jane rather wanted you to get on with clearing that patch near the summerhouse because she'll be sitting out there a lot if the weather keeps like this."

Garry nodded again, but instead of going away he picked up a cloth that lay on the hall table and began to polish the mirror.

"He's no intention of doing any gardening," said Bernard as he led Rosalind through a large kitchen and out to the lawn behind the house. "He's going to hang about in the hall until he thinks we are out of hearing and then he's going to burst into the sitting-room without knocking and demand that Jane stops making a fuss of Martin and makes a fuss of him instead. He's wildly jealous, as no doubt you have noticed."

Rosalind made no reply and they walked across the stretch of grass in silence. She was still seeing Martin's furiously indignant face, and the behaviour of the dumb boy seemed only a minor aggravation compared with the antagonism between her son and the man with whom she felt her own future to be inextricably linked.

8

The shed was a long low stone building with a sloping roof of mellowed tiles that looked as if it had at one time been a barn.

"I didn't need to do much with it," said Bernard. "The former owners had converted it into an annexe for their guests and it had water and electricity. It's my refuge and my joy. I love my shed. The moment I come through this door Bell House no longer exists for me."

"I expect that is a hint that you don't want me to say anything about what has just been happening," said Rosalind as she followed him into a low-ceilinged room full of books and comfortable chairs, "but I'm afraid I can't oblige. I can't possibly concentrate on any business until I've asked you why you had to behave like that to Jane and thus bear out her accusations against you."

"I feared you would say that," said Bernard. "Oh, well. Let's get it over with. Sit down and relax. I promise you there won't be any high drama here."

Rosalind took a chair. From where she sat she could see a booklined wall, a handsome rolltop desk open and overflowing with papers, and a white-painted closed door which presumably led to the kitchen. Bernard, sitting opposite her, faced the window from which there was a view across the lawn to the main house, and Rosalind noticed that he was constantly glancing out of the window as if to check that nobody was coming.

"So you think I'm being beastly to Jane," he said softly.

"Well." Rosalind paused a moment. "I wasn't exactly all that kind to her myself just now, but I'm rather ashamed of it. After all, there's no doubt that she's a sick woman. That panic at the meeting last week was genuine enough, and although she manages not to show it, I should think she's already had a lot to drink this afternoon."

"You're right," said Bernard. "It was taking place in the summer-house. A little private pub. She's not far off saturation point and it'll only take a few glasses for her to pass out. I'm surprised Martin hasn't noticed. He must know the symptoms."

"Martin hasn't noticed," said Rosalind, "because he is so angry with me that anything Jane does is all right. She needn't have bothered to work so hard at creating ill-feeling between us. It's there already. Martin and I have been having terrible rows about you."

"He thinks I'm a villain who is going to take his mother away from him and ruin her?"

"More or less. Quite a classic situation, isn't it? Hamlet and Oedipus and all that."

Bernard did not smile. "Martin's fears are very justified," he said. "I've dragged you into a very unpleasant situation."

"Nonsense. I put myself into it."

"That's not true, Rosalind. You were keeping yourself beautifully aloof from all personal involvement until I came along and tricked you into meeting Jane and hearing about our miseries."

"All right then, since honesty is the order of the day, yes, I was keeping aloof. But I couldn't have gone on like that much longer. Something or other was going to tip me off my perch at any moment and it just happened to be you. I take it you didn't engineer our meeting on the footpath to Leahurst?"

"No. That was pure chance."

"Then chance willed it that I should come tumbling down into the messiness and uncertainties of life again and here I am and nobody is to blame. So let's get back to the subject. Why did you have to speak like that to Jane just now? All you did was reinforce Martin in his bad opinion of you."

"It looks like that on the surface, I admit. But if you think about it you'll see it was the only line to take."

"I'm sorry. I don't see it at all," cried Rosalind. "All I can see is that he hates you like poison—hates you enough to poison you, since it's poison that's in all our minds—and that for me to live with Martin and be friends with you is going to be so difficult that I don't at the moment see how I am going to manage it at all."

"What shall we do, then? Chuck the whole thing in?"

"I've suggested that but Martin won't have it. He says I'll be resenting him for ever afterwards because he ruined my chances of getting my work more widely known. That's probably one reason, but the main reason is that he's determined to wipe you out. I mean wipe you out as far as I am concerned. Convince me so thoroughly that you are everything that is evil that I'll no longer be hankering after you, so to speak. That's what Martin is after, and since he knows he'll get no help from Deirdre because she's a thoroughly sensible and well-balanced girl, he's looking for another ally, and he's found one. The ideal ally for his purposes. And for Jane's too."

"Yes, it's an unholy alliance all right," said Bernard. "But there's nothing we can do about it at the moment except give Jane enough rope to hang herself—which incidentally was the purpose of my speech to her just now. She'll overdo it sooner or later, just as I said, and Martin's natural good sense will reassert itself."

"But I'm not so sure that it will!" cried Rosalind in despair. "I'm beginning to feel that I don't know him at all. Do you believe in inherited qualities? D'you think his father's weaknesses could be coming out in him? I'm frightened, Bernard. Yes, really frightened. Not that sickening apprehension I used to have all the time with John, but an awful overall fear. Like being lost in the fog. Or caught in a dark place with unseen enemies around."

"Oh Rosalind!" cried Bernard, stretching out his arms towards her. Then he leant back again, folded his arms, and said in a very determined manner: "No. Mustn't start that now. Things are quite complicated enough. Let me try to reassure you about Martin, at any rate. He knows all about alcoholism.

That's not likely to change. If he sees much more of Jane he'll see just how far gone she is in that direction. She's made a stupendous effort today and I admire her for it but she won't be able to keep it up. That'll cause a rift in the alliance. And then there's Garry."

"Yes, where does Garry come in? I was wondering about that."

"Garry worships Jane. He was brought up in an orphanage and was recommended for the job here by a former colleague of mine who is one of their governors. Jane is woman-ideal—mother, mistress, goddess—everything. That suits her fine, to have a household slave, but she does give something in return, as I said. She's taught him such speech as he's got. No one at the orphanage ever managed to get so far. But if you're worried about inheritance I don't think it's Martin you need have in mind. Heaven knows who Garry's parents were. He was found in a phone-box and they never traced anybody. As with all disabled people, the frustration sometimes overflows into violence, but unlike some of them he can't get rid of it by swearing, so he has to act instead. Chopping down the overgrown shrubbery has proved a useful outlet but there have been one or two occasions when he has gone for me. Not seriously and I've been able to handle it. So far as I know he has never raised a hand against Jane, but if she starts trying to show her power over him as she did just now, and which is a new game for her, then she probably won't remain immune much longer. So that's where Garry comes in," concluded Bernard. "Nice setting for a whodunit, isn't it? As if you and I hadn't had enough already of unnatural death in our lives!"

"Bernard," said Rosalind, "before we talk any more about anything, there's one thing that I must make absolutely clear."

"That you have no intention of embarking upon any sort of amorous adventure," he said quickly before she could speak further. "Yes, I think you have made that perfectly plain and I hope I have made it equally clear that I respect your wishes."

"That wasn't what I meant," said Rosalind. "I'm thinking of something more important. I told you what I thought of your character the other day and I haven't changed my opinion. I also told you that I didn't think you were a murderer or a potential murderer and I haven't changed my opinion about that either. But I'm not completely sure. That's what I think you ought to know straight away. That I don't entirely trust you in spite of what I've seen of Jane and what I think of Jane, and you mustn't think that I am always, in any circumstances whatever, going to be on your side because I'm not. I reserve the right to have my own opinion of you and to have my own suspicions of you if I see cause for them. That's all. I shan't mention it again but I wanted you to know."

"Thank you," said Bernard. "I should rather like to retaliate by giving you my opinion of you, but I don't think you want to hear it at the moment so I will only say I think you are a brave woman to agree to collaborate with a man whom you think capable of murder."

It was said in a perfectly serious voice but Rosalind could see from his expression that he was laughing at her. Nevertheless she was glad she had said what she did, even if his amusement did make her appear foolish, as if she had been caught out indulging in false heroics.

"All right," she said briskly. "As long as that's quite clear. How about having a look at the rest of the premises now?"

"Yes, I'm longing to show you my pride and joy," said Bernard, getting to his feet. And then he glanced out of the window yet again and said: "Damn. Here's Garry and no doubt fresh drama to follow. Our peace is gone."

"But he's alone," said Rosalind walking over to the window too. "Can't he look at things with us? It might give him some pleasure because he'll be able to hear me admiring everything."

"He's not going to be alone for long," said Bernard.

Even as he spoke they saw Jane and Martin emerge from the back door of the house and Jane take Martin's arm as they began to walk up the slight slope of the lawn.

"Damn," said Bernard again. "I had so much hoped to have the chance to show you my treasures in peace."

He sounded as disappointed as a small boy deprived of a treat and Rosalind felt moved to comfort him as she had often comforted Martin in like circumstances. But all she said was, "I'm sorry. That's my fault for insisting on talking first."

"Come on," said Bernard, suddenly grabbing her by the arm. "There's just time for a first impression."

They went through the white-painted door into a little lobby. "Back door, bathroom, store cupboard," said Bernard waving his free arm about. "Now shut your eyes."

Rosalind did so. She heard the click of a latch and then Bernard pushed her forward.

"Open Sesame," he said.

Rosalind gave a little gasp and cried with great warmth and sincerity: "Oh, what a lovely room!"

Bernard, still holding her arm, looked at her with equal pleasure. "Not Aladdin's cave," he said, "but I have done my best to make it look like an Elizabethan stillroom. The building lends itself, with the beams to hang drying herbs on and the open fireplace and the stone floor . . . I had to restore that, by the way. The previous owners had laid floor tiles. Understandable enough, since guests used this as a living-room as well as a kitchen."

"The table!" cried Rosalind. "What a perfectly gorgeous table!"

The long scrubbed deal table stood in the centre of the room. On it were shining copper pots and pans, wooden bowls, pottery jugs and other receptacles of various shapes and sizes, including a pestle and mortar.

"Mostly for show, I'm afraid," said Bernard. "Work is actually carried out here by the sink, where you see we have to step into our own era for convenience. There's a cupboard full of modern equipment by the electric cooker here, and the fridge comes in handy sometimes—"

He broke off and turned around. "Ah, here's Garry. I'll go and have a word with him. Look around as much as you like, Rosalind. I won't be long."

He shut the door behind him, leaving Rosalind temporarily absorbed in the twentieth-century corner of the kitchen. When he returned a few minutes later with Jane and Martin and Garry following close behind, Rosalind had got round to some shelves near the window. They were covered with jars and bottles and other containers of every conceivable shape and size.

"You're a bottle-collector too, I see," she said as the whole party came further into the room. "It seems to be quite a craze nowadays. There's a teacher at Martin's school who's got—how many is it, Martin?—five hundred?"

"Five hundred and fifty," said Martin in a tone of greater goodwill towards his mother than he had shown since they arrived at Bell House. "It's our chemistry teacher."

"You'd think he'd have had enough of bottles in the lab," said Jane. She was no longer tearful but her voice was rather too shrill and she moved around the kitchen in a jerky and nervous manner. To Rosalind's eyes, she was more like the anxious woman in the village hall than the confident beauty who had so dazzled Martin. Perhaps the effort had been too much for her; or perhaps her talk with Martin had not gone according to plan.

"The bottles are mostly for show too," said Bernard, "though I do use one occasionally when I actually decide to keep one of the recipes I have been trying out. In that case I always use one of the ridged bottles that chemists use for lotions and other preparations that are not to be taken internally. It's an additional safeguard against anybody taking something by mistake. You can't be too careful when you're messing about with the active ingredients of plants."

A safeguard for them but not for you, thought Rosalind. What's to stop one of the others from doping the harmless mixture you've made up for yourself and are keeping in a poison bottle to protect other people? She did not say this aloud, having decided that for the rest of this visit discretion was to be her policy, but the point seemed so obvious that she could not believe that the others were not aware of it too. Bernard was plainly leaning right over backwards to show how careful he was that nobody should come to any harm through his present interest in the power of plants. Was he building up his defence in advance because he believed that a tragedy was going to occur and he was going to be accused? Or was it all a sort of bluff, an exaggerated emphasis on his own precautions just because he was actually planning to poison Jane? A third possibility was that his remarks were to be interpreted as a warning to anybody who might be thinking of attempting anything.

"No, I don't extract the juice by crushing with pestle and mortar," Bernard was saying to Martin, who was showing a great interest in all the equipment. "That's the old way and very laborious too. I use the lazy modern method of liquidizers and juice extractors. There's a whole cupboard full of electrical gadgets here." And he opened the door that Rosalind had opened before the others arrived.

Jane moved forward and peered into the cupboard.

"You've got my liquidizer!" she cried, straightening up again and looking very flushed. "I thought you said you never took anything out of my kitchen."

Bernard knelt down to investigate the cupboard. There was a momentary silence that was broken by a strange growling animal sound. Rosalind felt a slight shock of revulsion and fear before she realized what it was, and for all Martin's noble declarations she was quite sure that he felt the same. It was Garry trying to speak.

"Isn't it the liquidizer from the kitchen in the house, Garry?" said Jane, turning to face the dumb boy.

The sounds stopped. He shook his head and made signs with his fingers that Jane seemed to understand. "Oh all right," she said. "I believe you. But I still think Bernard takes things out of the kitchen without asking. And it's just not true that he always puts anything he makes into a chemist's poison bottle. I went to use some vanilla essence the other day and it was lucky I smelt it because whatever it was in that bottle it certainly wasn't vanilla essence. I poured the whole lot away and made a lemon pudding instead."

Again there came a sound from Garry and this time it was Bernard who interrupted.

"If you were doubtful about the vanilla essence," he said, looking straight at Jane, "what you ought to have done was keep it and get it analysed. I've told you that before when you've made these suggestive remarks. You know exactly whom to approach and what to do if you have any suspicions. You never do it because you know perfectly well that the whole thing is a fabrication. Anybody can say that they didn't like the smell of something and therefore threw it away. It proves precisely nothing."

Jane began to cry. Martin looked at her with pity but made no move towards her and Rosalind suspected that Jane's behaviour was beginning to embarrass him. Perhaps Bernard had been right and that she had indeed overdone it as far as Martin was concerned. Garry, however, had no such inhibitions. Jane stretched out a hand to him and he took it and put his arm around her in a protective manner, just as Martin sometimes made the same gesture towards his mother.

"I'm sorry," said Bernard, turning to Rosalind and Martin and looking as if he really meant it, "to subject you to this domestic disagreement, but I really cannot stand this business of hinting and suggesting. I'm no more honest than the next man and I'm not much of a scientist but I do like to deal with facts rather than with suppositions whenever possible."

"So do I," said Martin, and he and Bernard met each other's eyes, which were much on a level. Not as friends, which Rosalind knew was too much to hope for, but as enemies who respect each other and know each other's strength.

"Good," said Bernard. "Then we know where we stand. Is there any question you would like to ask about my present work, Martin? If so, I promise to give you a factual answer. Whether you believe it or not is your own affair."

"I'd like to ask," said Martin, "whether if you extracted the juice from fresh leaves or stalks of hemlock, it would taste so strong or so vile that nobody could possibly drink it by mistake."

"I don't think it's quite fair, Martin," began Rosalind, but Bernard interrupted her.

"Yes, that's a perfectly fair question. And it will receive as factual an answer as I can give. You could certainly extract such a juice without difficulty and it would contain an appreciable amount of coniine—about two per cent, I think. I forget the average percentage but I could look it up if you really want to know. This, as you no doubt know, is a strong alkaline poison with an antispasmodic and sedative action when used in medicinally approved quantities, but with a paralysing and even fatal action when the dose is exceeded. I can't tell you the fatal dose for a human being. I should have to look that up too, but as far as I recollect a very few drops can be fatal to a small animal, and children have been poisoned simply by making whistles out of the hollow stems of the hemlock plant. Does it taste vile? I've never drunk any hemlock juice so I can't speak from experience in this case, but judging from the smell I should think it probably tastes revolting and that nobody could drink it neat without knowing it. Whether the taste would be disguised by some strong spirit—rum, sloe gin, something like that, again I can't say and I don't propose to experiment, nor do I advise anybody else to. As again you no doubt know, the effect of alcohol of any kind is greatly to increase the power of any drug with which it is combined, so a mixture of hemlock juice and rum or brandy, for example, would be even more lethal than hemlock juice on its own. Does that answer your question, Martin?"

Bernard could seldom, thought Rosalind, have had a more attentive audience. She herself was listening with a mixture of horror and fascination. Martin was listening as if it were a lecture that he needed to memorize in order to pass an exam. Jane and Garry both had their eyes on Bernard's face, Jane with a look of fear that Rosalind suspected was partly assumed, and Garry with an inscrutable expression in his dark eyes.

"Thanks, yes, I think it does answer it," said Martin. "As you say, I can look up the percentages if I really want to know more exactly. But I've got another question if you don't mind."

"Fire away."

"If one really wanted to introduce the juice from some poisonous plant into somebody's food or drink so that they didn't notice it, is there any such plant that doesn't have too strong a taste?"

"Martin, this really is going too far!" exclaimed Rosalind.

"It's a question that can receive a factual answer," said Martin stubbornly.

"It can indeed," said Bernard, "but again I have to emphasize that I am no expert and that I am simply quoting what I have read on the subject for myself. And I think that covers your objection, Rosalind. If I can look up these facts, so can anybody else. They do not need to depend on me for the information. So to answer your question, I would say that the hemlock water dropwort is just such a plant. The yellow juice that comes from the stem and the root is a virulent poison, even more potent than the juice of the hemlock proper and with, so far as I know, no antidote. And apparently—but here again I speak only from hearsay because I do not propose to experiment on myself—the taste is sweetish and by no means unpleasant. Hence the numerous cases of cattle poisoned by eating the roots. It has been used as a rat poison. As with hemlock, the effect is a paralysing one."

"Isn't that the plant," cried Jane, "that they call 'Dead Tongue' because it paralyses the speech?"

There were several seconds of complete silence while Jane, looking pleased with herself as if by coming out with this piece of folklore she had scored a point over her husband, stared at Bernard, and Bernard himself, together with Rosalind and Martin, very deliberately refrained from looking at Garry.

The silence became more and more unbearable: Jane's remark hung in the atmosphere like a threatening cloud. Rosalind held her breath, and then found it difficult to breathe at all.

At last it dawned on Jane what she had said.

"Oh, my God!"

She clapped both hands to her mouth and turned to look at Garry. "Oh heavens! How could I have forgotten! I just didn't think. Oh Garry, I'm so sorry. I simply didn't think. I deserve to be dosed with hemlock water dropwort myself for being such a tactless fool. Please Garry. Forgive me."

She stretched out her arms to him. He brushed her aside and ran out of the room and a moment later they heard the back door of the shed bang behind him.

— 9 —

"I didn't think," said Jane, looking appealingly at each one of the others in turn. "I honestly had forgotten for the moment."

Rosalind was inclined to believe Jane in this, if in nothing else. "I know," she muttered. "Things just slip out."

"God knows what he'll do now," said Bernard gloomily. "Trample down half the herb garden, I expect."

"Or smash my best tea service," said Jane. "It was china last time, if you remember."

"I remember all right," said Bernard. "And invaluable though Garry is in many ways, I'm beginning to wonder whether it's worth it."

"But Bernie, we can't get rid of him. It's his only home."

Jane was still speaking without a trace of affectation. She sounded anxious, but that was natural enough in the circumstances. And Bernard was speaking quite naturally too. During this brief interchange there was a temporary truce in the warfare between husband and wife: they had become two people with a common problem to worry about.

"I suppose you'd better go and try to soothe him down," said Bernard.

Jane looked more frightened than ever. "He might go for me," she said.

"Shall I go?" suggested Martin.

That's directed at Bernard and me, thought Rosalind. It's to show how compassionate he is towards both Jane and Garry, how lacking in sympathy I am myself, and how cowardly Bernard is. As she thought this she reflected that this sort of coldly dispassionate analysis of Martin's motives was something quite new in her. The rift between them had indeed gone very deep.

"It's not a bad idea," said Bernard. "You're more likely than any of the rest of us to get the better of him in a punch-up."

"I don't want to fight him," snapped Martin. "I want to help him."

"Don't we all," said Bernard. "Unfortunately our motives are sometimes misunderstood."

They stared at each other and the antipathy between them flared up again.

"Well, if you're going you'd better get on with it," said Rosalind impatiently. "Where's Garry likely to have gone?"

Nobody answered.

"I'll find him!" cried Martin, and rushed out of the building by the back door, banging it as Garry had done.

After he had gone a noticeable change came over Jane. It was as if she had stopped making any effort. The voice was different and the whole body seemed to slump.

"I've got to have a drink after that," she said, making for the door. "No need for you two to come. Why don't you get down to your own business? There's a nice comfy divan in the other room here and nobody's likely to interrupt."

And she laughed loudly, as she had done in the car park outside the village hall.

"I could also do with a drink," said Bernard. "And I dare say Rosalind could too. We'll all go back to the house. I don't keep any booze out here," he added to Rosalind.

"No booze," said Jane as they left the building. "Only hemlock juice. That was a very fascinating lecture you gave us all. Wasn't it, Rosalind? A little lesson in murder." She laughed again. "I wonder which one of us will take it up?"

Neither Bernard nor Rosalind made any reply. When they got back to the sitting-room in Bell House he produced glasses and some bottles from the carved oak corner cupboard that Rosalind had noticed and admired when they first came into the room.

"Sherry? Whiskey? Gin? Miss Lesley Green's elderberry wine, of which I was given a bottle last week?"

"I think I'd like some of the elderberry," said Rosalind. "Lesley gave me some too. It's very good."

Bernard poured it out and handed her the glass. "I'll join you," he said. "How about you, Jane?"

"Me? No, thanks. Not for me. Don't seem to fancy anything made from plants. Funny, isn't it? I'll have some gin."

Bernard picked up a large unopened bottle of gin and Jane immediately snatched it from him. "I'll do it myself," she said.

"As you like," he replied indifferently. Then he added with that note in his voice that always swung Rosalind over to Jane's side again: "Incidentally, gin is made from a plant too. From the juniper. You're going to be rather hard put to it to find an alcoholic drink that is not made from some sort of plant."

"I know that," snapped Jane after she had drunk down one glass at a gulp and was pouring another. "I shouldn't have said plants. I meant home-made stuff. I don't mind so long as it comes from a factory. And so long as I open the bottle myself." She drank again and poured out yet another glass.

"Do you propose," said Bernard, "to ensure that you always get an unopened bottle by throwing away the remainder or by drinking it all at one go?"

Rosalind, sipping the elderberry wine that was indeed delicious, felt herself wincing inwardly at the cutting note in his voice. Bernard's attraction for her was becoming so strong that it was painful to her to hear him being so hurtful, even though it was not directed at herself. And whatever Jane's faults and misdeeds, there was no doubt that she was a woman who badly needed help and was not getting much from her husband.

Jane made no reply except to refill her glass yet again.

"Martin wouldn't like it if he saw you," said Bernard. "You've done so well with him so far. It's a pity to spoil it now."

Rosalind could not bear any more of this. "I'm getting worried about Martin," she broke in. "I'm afraid he's likely to do more harm than good to that poor boy. I think one of us had better go and try to find them."

"Jane perhaps?" said Bernard.

Both he and Rosalind looked at Jane, who had sat down in the chair in which she had been sitting earlier, and was raising the glass to her lips once more, frowning with concentration as if it were the most important thing in the world. The level in the gin bottle was getting very low.

"You make me sick," said Rosalind to Bernard in a soft voice.

"Do you think I haven't tried to stop it?" he replied equally quietly. "I expect you tried to stop John Bannister, didn't you?"

"I'm going to look for the boys," said Rosalind abruptly, and left the room.

After she had gone Bernard walked over to Jane's chair, took the glass from her hand, pulled her to her feet, and said briskly: "Come on. You'd better go to bed."

"Hemlock . . ." murmured Jane.

"Gin," said Bernard firmly. "You can have the rest of it upstairs. Here's the bottle. Don't drop it."

They moved to the door, across the hall, and up the stairs with Bernard half-carrying Jane and Jane clutching the gin bottle with both hands and alternately laughing and muttering. Rosalind, coming back into the hall from the kitchen after changing her mind about going in search of Martin, saw them at the turn of the stairs and hastily returned to the kitchen again because she felt sure that they would rather she did not look. It was a big well-equipped kitchen with a pleasant view up the gentle slope of the lawn to the line of shrubs beyond. At one end of the bushes and partly concealed by them was the shed: at the other end was the little white-painted summer-house.

The trolley containing the tea things stood untouched near the sink. Rosalind moved the used crockery on to the draining-board and began to wash up. It was a relief to be doing something useful and straightforward after all the emotional ups and downs of the afternoon, and washing-up had the advantage that she could look out of the window. She had nearly finished when she saw Martin. He came round the side of the summer-house and walked along the edge of the lawn as if he were going to go straight round to the front of Bell House.

Rosalind wiped her hands quickly and went out to intercept him.

"No luck?" she said.

Martin looked hot and tired and not pleased to see her. "I don't think he wants to be found," he said. "I've been all over the place. I saw him going into the shed a few minutes ago, but I didn't see where he'd come from and by the time I got to the shed myself there was no sign of him."

"Perhaps he's hiding in the shrubbery," said Rosalind. Then she added in a different tone of voice: "What's the matter? Have you got that rash again?"

Martin was wearing his best jeans and a light cotton shirt that was much looser than his usual skimpy wear. His right hand kept pulling at the front of this shirt as if something were irritating him.

"Don't fuss, Mum," he snapped. "I'm just hot, that's all. I'm sick of this place. D'you think I can go home?"

"I don't see why not," said Rosalind. "I'll make your apologies to Bernard. He's putting Jane to bed at the moment. She's not well."

"Not well?" Martin had moved away, but he turned round again at these words.

"I assure you she has not been poisoned," said Rosalind. "At any rate, not in the way you are thinking of. For heaven's sake, Martin, do try to recover your common sense. Suppose for argument that Bernard does want to get rid of her. Do you seriously think he is going to go out of his way to give us all a lecture on poisonous plants and the way they work and then immediately go and pop some already prepared hemlock juice into her drink? You'd have to be practically half-witted to do anything so obvious and whatever Bernard is, he's not half-witted."

"It could be a sort of double bluff," muttered Martin, pulling at the front of his shirt again.

"You've been reading too many whodunits," said Rosalind, "where it does turn out to be the most likely person after all. Personally I think Bernard was getting so fed up with Jane's accusations and your barely veiled suspicions that he decided the best thing was to bring it all out into the open and show just how easy it would be to poison somebody that way. Then if anything ever did happen he'd have all these witnesses to say that he wasn't doing any secret plotting but was talking quite freely, which would tell in his favour."

"Exactly," cried Martin. "He's clever. Just as you said. He made damn sure we all knew what to do."

"And whose fault was that? It was you who was asking the questions."

"He wanted me to ask them," said Martin sullenly. "He'd have got you to if I hadn't done it. Or needled Jane so much that she asked them herself."

Rosalind was rather startled by these last remarks of Martin's. Her mind had been very busy with the conversation that had taken place in the kitchen of the shed and she had more or less come to the same conclusion—that Bernard had been determined to impart some vital information about poisonous plants—but she had not expected Martin to be so perceptive in the emotional state he had been in.

"I still think Bernard was trying to protect himself against any possible accusation," she said firmly after a moment's pause.

"Just what I said," replied Martin. "To make himself such an obvious suspect that nobody could possibly suspect."

Rosalind gave a little laugh. "Aren't we being a little premature? Nobody's been poisoned, and we've no serious reason to suppose that anyone is going to be. It's all speculation. All that's happened is that we've had a rather embarrassing tea-party and Jane has made a tactless remark that upset Garry and he's probably gone for a long walk to get over it. Incidentally," she went on as Martin made a little angry impatient sound, "if you're looking for a murderer I'd have thought Garry was your man. He's had a miserable afternoon. First of all he sees Jane cooing over you, then he's sent out of the room. Then he sees her making eyes at you again—a nice-looking boy who's quite normal, who's got nothing wrong with him and who's got a voice. And then she comes out with that frightful remark . . . Yes, I think Garry would make a very good suspect indeed. There must be no end of bitterness and frustration locked up in him and he's got access to all the equipment in the shed and knows all about poisonous plants. You'd better look out, Martin. He obviously thinks of you as a rival. You may be the one he's planning to do away with, not Jane."

As soon as she had finished speaking Rosalind knew that she had made matters even worse between Martin and herself. She had intended to speak light-heartedly, to appeal to his sense of humour and proportion and lower the tension between them, but instead of this she had merely sounded sarcastic. She could actually recognize in her own voice the sort of tone that had sometimes driven John Bannister to violence and she was frightened and distressed, but not altogether surprised, when Martin glared at her in a manner very reminiscent of his father.

"Who's doing the speculating now?" he demanded. "Those last remarks of yours are positively slanderous. And positively obscene. To accuse someone of murder because he's had a rotten deal in life and is disabled and can't speak for himself . . ."

"I'm sorry," said Rosalind. "I shouldn't have said that."

"Anyway, what's the matter with Jane?" he asked, not mollified at all, but speaking very aggressively.

Rosalind hesitated for a moment. Her impulse was to hit back at Martin with the truth: Jane's drinking herself silly with gin, making up for lost time during that show she put on for you this afternoon. Her hesitation was twofold: it contained pity for both Martin and Jane. And in any case, she thought, there can be no more truth now between Martin and me: we've lost something very precious and it may never return. As this thought flashed through Rosalind's mind a terrible sense of desolation came over her. To lose Martin, her son, her comfort and her friend, and all because on a bright June morning when the life force was stirring in her again she had met a man in the field who had talked and acted in a way that had roused from its half-death her half-buried self . . .

"Jane has this nervous illness, Martin," she said aloud. "I told you about it. It's a terrific effort for her to be with people at all. I think she did wonderfully well this afternoon and she was bound to suffer from a reaction afterwards."

"She told me after you'd gone out to the shed—" began Martin, and then stopped. "No, I don't think I'd better repeat it," he added a moment later. "It was said in confidence. But it wasn't what you and Bernard thought she was going to tell me, I'll say that much. I'd like to have seen her again before I go but I suppose that's impossible."

"I'm afraid so," said Rosalind.

"Oh well. It doesn't matter. We'll be in touch. I've promised to come and sit with her now and then. She's terribly lonely. I'm going now. Will you be long?"

"I don't know," replied Rosalind. "I think I'd better wait till Garry turns up. And I'm also supposed to be making some arrangements about the painting."

"Then I don't suppose you'll be home for at least another hour," said Martin. "I'll make myself some supper if I want anything."

"I thought you were going out with Deirdre."

Martin made an impatient noise. "Deirdre and I aren't committed to each other," he snapped. "We don't have to live in each other's pockets. You won't be home for another hour, then?"

It was said insistently, almost aggressively. Pity for Deirdre, combined with a feeling that she had had enough of Bell House for the time being, almost caused Rosalind to change her mind and come with him. The thought of the little cottage by the church, even with Martin sulking upstairs, was very enticing. It was one thing alone that in the end held her back: the tone of her own remark to Bernard when he had been lashing out at Jane. "You make me sick," she had said, and she had been wishing ever since that she had not said it. Of course his attitude towards Jane was horrible but that didn't mean he didn't suffer. Who should know that better than Rosalind herself? There had been many an occasion when she had spoken to John Bannister in such a way that if other people had been present they might well have cried out, "You make me sick." Even at the cost of further estrangement from Martin, and whatever the future might hold, Rosalind felt that she could not leave Bell House this day without letting Bernard know that she understood.

"I doubt if I'll be home in much less than an hour," she said to Martin.

Without saying another word he turned and walked away round the side of the house and Rosalind looked after him. He was moving quickly but stiffly, with his arms held almost straight by his sides, and not rushing along with all four limbs all over the place as he usually did. She watched him until he was out of sight, and the thought came to her as if it had been spoken by another voice than her own: "He's walking out of your life." She had the feeling that in not accompanying Martin now she had made a great decision; that in looking back on this moment she would say to herself—that was the turning point, that was your best chance to stop it; that was the path you did not take.

Yet surely it could not matter all that much. She and her son had lost their friendship and their trust in each other, and it was going to be a long time before they regained it. If ever. One little hour more or less could hardly make much difference.

10

After Martin had gone Rosalind returned to the kitchen and finished the washing-up. Bernard had not yet come downstairs, and she decided to go back to the shed to see if Garry was there. Martin had said he wasn't, but he might not have looked properly, or the dumb boy might have come in meanwhile through the back door. On the telephone table in the hall of Bell House lay a pad for messages, and Rosalind scribbled a note for Bernard and propped it up against the phone.

There was no sign of Garry in the big booklined room in the shed, but as Rosalind opened the white door that led to the rest of the building she had the impression that somebody had just made some movement behind it. The lobby too was empty, however, and she pushed open the door of the stillroom with a sense of unease amounting almost to apprehension, as if it were something supernatural that she was in danger of encountering, and not simply an unfortunate and unhappy human creature.

The big kitchen, with its mixture of sweet and pungent scents and its many shelves and cupboards and objects of all kinds, seemed very much a place of life and activity. But to Rosalind in her present mood it felt sinister as well—a sort of sorcerer's cell. She looked around carefully, but unless Garry was hiding in one of the cupboards—and they were crammed so tight that there would not be space for him—he was not in here either.

She was about to give up and return to Bell House, where

surely Bernard would have finished seeing Jane to bed by now, when it occurred to her that she could save them yet another trip to the shed if she collected the plant specimens from the refrigerator herself. The idea was that she should draft out a few specimen colour plates, each containing one poisonous plant and one or more harmless ones, for submission to the publishers. Bernard had assured her that it was purely a formality and that the contract was hers; nevertheless Rosalind was determined to make as good a job of it as she possibly could.

To paint some really good illustrations was a worthwhile aim, and above all, it was something solid and practical to hold on to in all the miserable muddle of the afternoon and the wreck of her relationship with her son. She made her way slowly round the long deal table to where the big refrigerator stood in the corner near the sink and stretched out her hand to open it. Before she could touch it she felt her wrist caught and held, just as it had been a few days previously when with rather stupid bravado she had raised the leaf of the hemlock plant to her lips.

This time the shock of surprise was much greater because Rosalind had believed herself to be alone and had not heard anybody moving behind her. The hand holding her wrist was not Bernard's. A trained artist's eye and a good visual memory enabled her to see that at a glance. Nor was it Martin's hand, although it was not unlike it in size and shape. It was a boy's hand, with a great deal of nervous strength in it, but unlike Martin's, the nails were bitten to the quick.

By the time Rosalind turned round and spoke she knew who it was she was going to see, but she still felt this unreasoning fear, as if of something not quite human, when she looked into the dumb boy's face.

"You startled me, Garry," she said with a smile. "Why mayn't I open the fridge?"

Garry dropped her wrist and stared at her without making any attempt to communicate, and Rosalind mentally kicked herself for her stupidity in asking him a question that could not be answered with a shake or a nod.

"Mr. Goodwin said the plants I was to draw were keeping

fresh in the fridge," went on Rosalind hurriedly. "But I'd better wait till he comes himself. He shouldn't be long."

She moved away from the modern corner of the room and began to inspect some of the articles on the long table, picking up things at random and putting them down again as she commented.

"What a lovely chopping-board—there's nothing nicer than wood . . . I've always loved wooden spoons . . ."

She was talking quickly, nervously, and incessantly, as if it were essential that there should be the sound of a human voice in the room, as if silence meant danger.

"I like this jug. A measuring jug, I suppose."

Rosalind picked it up as she spoke. Her progress along the side of the table had now brought her near the door, but Garry had kept pace with her, three feet away at the other side of the table, stopping when she stopped, moving on when she did, not touching anything or attempting to stop her from her obsessional handling of objects, but staring at her with those dark eyes whose expression was impossible to read.

"It's a beautiful jug," went on Rosalind, "much too good to use just for measuring. But I can't read what sort of measures they are. How much does it hold?"

Again she could have bitten her tongue in annoyance with herself for asking a question that could not be answered, and she hurriedly went on: "But of course you don't use these things here . . . the stuff you use is all in the cupboards . . ."

The end of the table now. Under Rosalind's endless flow of talk she was wondering how long it would take her to get used to being with a speechless human being, and feeling a reluctant admiration for Jane who, whatever her motives, had obviously managed to accommodate herself to Garry's defect and had given the boy some human contact. Rosalind felt that she would not have been capable of it herself, and since she had always believed herself to be a compassionate sort of person, the thought made her ashamed. She was feeling not only frightened, but also depressed by the time she reached the door at last.

Garry continued to stare at her as she pushed open the kitchen door. Rosalind was convinced that he could read her thoughts and that the expression in his eyes was now one of contempt. This silent undermining of her own self-respect, following on the uncanny fear and the shock of being arrested as she was about to open the door of the refrigerator, worked on Rosalind's already overstrained nerves to such an extent that when she saw Bernard coming in at the back door of the shed she rushed towards him as if he had come to rescue her.

He put an arm round her and said briskly, like a stereotype of a police constable: "Hullo-ullo-ullo! What's all this, now?"

"Nothing," said Rosalind. "Sorry."

She tried to pull away but Bernard held her back. "You're all of a tremble. As if you'd seen a ghost. A ghost in the stillroom. I say, that's rather a good title for a thriller. Or a Gothic novel. Pity I'm not that sort of a writer."

"I thought I'd collect the plants," said Rosalind, ignoring these pleasantries, "but Garry said . . . I mean he didn't say, but he stopped me from opening the fridge, and I rather gathered . . ."

She broke off, appalled at herself yet again. It was as if there were some demon in control of her speech, prompting her to keep calling attention to Garry's disability.

"I'm sorry," she said again in a helpless way, and looked up to see Garry standing in the door of the kitchen, staring at Bernard and herself with the same fixed intensity as he had followed her progress down the kitchen table.

It seemed to Rosalind now that there was hostility as well as contempt in the boy's eyes, violent hostility towards both Bernard and herself. She suddenly became very conscious that Bernard's arm was still round her shoulders and this time she did pull herself right away.

Bernard took a couple of steps towards the mute boy.

"What's the matter, Garry?" he asked. "Write it down for me. You've got your pad and pencil?"

Garry inclined his head slightly.

"Then I'd like to know why you stopped Mrs. Bannister taking the plant specimens out of the fridge," said Bernard. "You know perfectly well they are for her to paint. I told you so when we picked them. Hurry up, now. Get out your writing-pad and let me know what it's all about."

Bernard's voice was authoritative but not unkind. Rosalind wondered whether he was aware of the boy's hostility towards him.

Garry did not extract the writing materials from his pocket, but took hold of Bernard by the arm and began to pull him towards the door of the kitchen.

"You want me to come and see something?" asked Bernard.

Again Garry bent his head.

"All right, then. Come on, Rosalind. I've no idea what it is, but I don't expect it'll bite. That's one thing to be said for the study of plants. They may poison you if you're so stupid as to make a mistake, but they don't sting you or bite you, like insects or animals. Unless, of course, you're competing for a lavender bush with an angry bee."

Rosalind was grateful for his attempts to introduce a little light relief, although she still felt too shaken and apprehensive to respond to them. When they reached the far end of the kitchen Bernard put his hand on the door of the refrigerator and turned to face Garry.

"You've not put a bomb in here by any chance, have you?"

It was said in the same joking tone of voice, but Rosalind had a feeling that Bernard was a little apprehensive himself.

Garry shook his head.

"Quite sure?" said Bernard, still holding the door closed.

Garry nodded vigorously.

"Well, if you have, it's going to blow you up too," said Bernard, "which I take it you don't want to happen. So I think I'll believe you. Anyway, here goes."

He pulled open the door of the big refrigerator. Rosalind felt a distinct sense of relief when nothing happened, and she had the impression that Bernard felt it too. There was very little to be seen on the shelves.

"We don't really need it in here," said Bernard, "but we'd bought a new one for the house and it seemed a pity to get rid of this. Occasionally it's useful to cool something off quickly or keep something fresh—like the plants. They'd have been all right outside for a day or two, but they're safer in here, and as we've got it . . ."

He broke off and stooped to peer at the bottom shelf.

"That's funny. I thought we put them down there. There

were six specimens, big ones mostly, each labelled round the stem. They were all in the same jar with a plastic bag put over them. Has it got pushed to the back?" He felt about inside the refrigerator for a moment and then straightened up and said, "Well I'm damned! They're gone. Plastic bag and all. Here's the jar. This is a bit of a nuisance. I'll have to collect a fresh lot. Pity. I'd chosen the samples very carefully to show their characteristics."

He closed the door of the refrigerator and turned to Garry.

"I suppose that was what you wanted to tell me?"

Garry nodded.

"You didn't take them out yourself by any chance?"

Garry shook his head.

"I suppose I've got to believe you," said Bernard, "since I can't think of any reason why you'd want to remove them. You wouldn't need those specimens even if you were thinking of squeezing out a bit of hemlock juice because you know perfectly well where you can pick plenty more of the stuff and no one's keeping track of your movements so you can do what you damn well like. You're sure you didn't move those specimens, Garry?"

Bernard repeated the question in what to Rosalind seemed an almost threatening manner. The boy simply shook his head again and Rosalind could have sworn that he was telling the truth. But he knew they'd gone, she added mentally to herself; that's why he stopped me.

She glanced at Garry and saw that he was taking his pad and pencil from his pocket. While he was writing, Rosalind and Bernard exchanged glances but said nothing. Then Garry handed Bernard the slip of paper. He read it and passed it on to Rosalind. It was written in a childish but clear and legible hand.

> You told me nobody was to take them out but
> yourself. I wanted ice-cubes for my headache and
> saw they were gone. About half an hour ago.

"Half an hour," said Rosalind aloud. She tried to think back over the events of the last half-hour. Bernard taking Jane upstairs; herself washing the tea-things in the kitchen at Bell House; a few minutes talking to Martin in the garden; washing up again; coming to the shed; the meeting with Garry; herself talking and talking, nervously, endlessly, as she and Garry moved along the opposite sides of the long table; and finally Bernard to the rescue.

These were roughly her own recollections of the past half-hour and somewhere among them was a tantalizing memory that she couldn't quite grasp but that she felt could be important. Only a little thing. Her mind nearly caught at it and then it slipped away again.

Meanwhile Bernard had asked Garry another question and another slip of paper was in use.

"You told me nobody else was to go to the fridge," Garry had written.

"I don't think you heard me," said Bernard to Rosalind. "I asked him why he stopped you opening it since he knew the plants were gone. All right, Garry." He turned back to the boy. "I'm not criticizing you. It's quite true that I told you not to let anyone take anything from the fridge and you weren't to know that Mrs. Bannister is an exception because she is going to be working with me as artist."

Had the boy had the power of speech, Rosalind felt sure that he would have used it now. Once again she could sense in him that silent hostility towards both Bernard and herself. But whether it was because, in spite of Jane's tactlessness, he still adored Jane and saw in Rosalind a threat to her; or whether it was because his jealousy of Martin extended to Martin's mother, Rosalind could not tell. She only knew that Garry hated her and that it was a hatred all the more frightening in that it could never be spoken.

"So the ban does not apply to Mrs. Bannister in future," Bernard was saying. "Only to other visitors. And we'll be more careful about keeping this place locked up in future. It's locked at night, of course," he explained to Rosalind, "but when Garry and I are in and out of it during the day we don't always bother. I suppose you've no idea who might have got the plants?" he added casually, addressing Garry.

The boy didn't write anything more but lifted his hand and pointed a finger straight at Bernard.

"Me? You mean you thought I'd taken them myself?"

Garry nodded and let his hand fall back to his side.

"Well, that's just damn silly," said Bernard. "If you thought I'd taken them out myself why the hell did you stage this little surprise opening-up just now?"

Garry made no movement to write, but stood staring sullenly at the floor. Bernard glared at him, glanced at Rosalind equally angrily, and then back to the boy.

"Ah, I see," he said slowly at last. "Or rather, I think I do. It's all part of the Bernard-Goodwin-is-going-to-poison-his-wife act, isn't it?"

Garry did not stir.

"That's it," went on Bernard. "You've either taken the plants yourself or you know perfectly well who has taken them. This little comedy was all put on for the benefit of Mrs. Bannister. It's meant to work round to having her suspect me of being up to some dirty business. Or else having me suspect her. One or the other. It's all too subtle and complicated for me. In that case it's obviously pointless to enquire further into the disappearance of the plants because I'm obviously not going to get the truth. What I'd like to know is, did you think this up by yourself? Or did Jane put you up to it? And was this little bit of drama early on in the drawing-room all part of it? No, it's all right. Don't trouble to get your writing-pad out again. I can't be bothered with any more lies and excuses. I've a bloody good mind to clear out completely right now and leave the two of you to get on with it. Jane and you. Or the three of you, if Martin's in it too."

Rosalind, listening intently and anxiously to Bernard's angry voice, gave a little start at the sound of Martin's name.

"Except that there'd be no point in that either," Bernard stormed up, "because if I flew off to New York tonight you'd still hang it on me somehow. There'd be hemlock juice turning up in something Jane was just about to drink and the whole lot of you would be swearing blind that I'd put it there before I ran away. So that's no good either. I just can't win, can I? Very well then, Garry."

Bernard lowered his voice. There was a cold threat in it now
that sounded to Rosalind more alarming than his previous loud
fury.

"Very well. If that's how it is, let me warn you now. You
and Jane can play your little tricks on me and do your
damnedest. I'm used to them. I've survived them before and
I'll survive them again. But you're not to drag Mrs. Bannister
into it. I'm warning you now. If you pull her into it in any way
at all, then you're finished. I'll do for you. You know perfectly
well what I mean. And don't worry to tell Jane. I'll tell her for
myself. I mean it. If there's so much as a whisper of talk about
Mrs. Bannister, then that's the end of you, Garry."

The boy raised his eyes from the floor at last and stared at
Bernard, but whether in fear or in defiance Rosalind could not
tell. All she knew was that Bernard's words had struck her very
cold, and the shiver was for her own sake and not for Garry's.

"Clear out now," said Bernard, "and go and get yourself a
meal if you feel like it. I don't want anything to eat and I doubt
if Jane will. She's been swigging gin and I doubt if she'll be
much in evidence again today. Go on. I want to lock up myself
this evening and I want to talk to Mrs. Bannister too."

"Garry," said Rosalind in a low voice as the boy seemed
reluctant to move. "Garry. I'm sorry if you feel my presence is
in some way a threat to you. Or if it upsets you. I can only
swear that I never intended it. I never even knew of your
existence until you opened the door this afternoon. I certainly
don't wish you any ill. Nor Jane either. I wish you nothing but
good. And to show that I do, I'm going to say goodbye to you
now and to promise you that you won't be seeing me at this
house again. Nor in the village for very much longer. My son
and I will move as soon as we possibly can, and I'll be right out
of your life. I can't say more than that, Garry, except that I'm
very sorry indeed that you've been caused this distress and I'd
like to wish you all the very best for your future."

Rosalind held out her hand. It had cost her a great effort to
make this speech, but she felt she had to attempt a reconciliation straight away, and at the moment of speaking, her words
were sincerely meant.

Her hand remained open and offered for the best part of half a minute. Garry made not the slightest move to take it.

"I'm sorry," said Rosalind at last. "Very sorry indeed. I wish you well."

Garry's dark eyes glared at her and Garry's speechless mouth opened and shut. Rosalind felt as if she were being silently cursed. Then the boy turned and ran out of the back door of the shed.

— 11 —

"I meant that," said Rosalind, following Bernard into the booklined room after he had locked the kitchen and the back door. "After this last business I am quite determined to leave Swallowfields, whatever Martin says. He can stay here on his own if he likes. I'm going."

"I can appreciate your feelings," replied Bernard formally, "and I can only say I am very sorry indeed to have exposed you to this."

"Oh, don't be silly. You didn't expose me. I exposed myself to it. I'd never have got myself involved with you and your affairs at all if I hadn't been in the mood to get involved. But it's gone too far. I'm bitterly disappointed about the job. I'd have loved to do it, and I think we'd have worked well together. But it isn't worth it if it means some sort of unpleasantness that could bring you or me under suspicion. I must say, though," added Rosalind, "that the idea that Garry and Jane are planning to have you accused of trying to poison Jane does sound rather fantastic."

"You think I'm imagining it all? You don't think, after what you've seen and heard this afternoon, that it could be true?"

"I suppose it could be all talk and no action," said Rosalind.

"Garry can't talk," said Bernard shortly. "You'd better say all thought and no action. So you think I'm making an unnecessary fuss?"

Rosalind shook her head.

"It must be very disagreeable," said Bernard in his most ironic manner, "to believe that somebody in your household is trying to poison you. But I assure you that it is equally disagreeable to believe that somebody is trying to get you accused of trying to poison them. When it comes to a feeling of utterly helpless apprehension, I imagine there is very little to choose between the two cases."

"All right, then," said Rosalind. "Why don't you just clear out yourself as you suggested?"

"I gave you the reason."

"Jane told me you'd never divorce because you don't want to have to pay her any money."

"That's a lie. Obviously she'd bleed me white over the alimony, but that's not the reason. I don't want a divorce for the same reason as I married her. I'm sorry for her. More than ever now. You of all people ought to know about sticking to a partner whom you despise because you can't help feeling sorry for them."

It was said in a thoroughly unkind manner, but Rosalind did not feel hurt. He's hurting himself more than the other person when he talks like this, she told herself dispassionately.

"So you won't leave Jane," she said aloud. "What about Garry? What did you mean by saying you'd finish him if he tried to drag me in?"

"I didn't mean I was going to murder him, if that's what you're worried about."

Rosalind sat down on the arm of a chair. She was still quite determined that this was to be the last time she would ever talk to Bernard Goodwin and she was trying hard to stifle the regrets and the emptiness that would keep welling up and to collect her thoughts sufficiently to find out a few things she badly wanted to know.

"What did you mean, then?" she asked.

"It's of no interest to you if you are never going to see any of us again," said Bernard.

"All right, but there is something that I think I've a right to know, since I may well be personally involved if your suspicions are correct."

"About those plants disappearing," said Bernard immediately.

It was extraordinary, thought Rosalind, how their minds seemed to move in the same direction, how they picked up each other's thoughts even before they were uttered, and she was conscious of a great stab of regret that insisted on making itself felt. If only she and Bernard could have met and got to know each other in different circumstances . . .

"Yes, about those specimens," she said briskly. "What exactly had you collected for me to draw?"

Bernard answered in the same businesslike manner. "Hemlock, cow parsley, and wild carrot. Hemlock water dropwort and water fennel. And a particularly nice little foxglove."

"How dangerous are they? I mean," went on Rosalind quickly, "would it be possible to extract enough poison from one or more of these specimens to do serious damage?"

"In certain circumstances, yes, it would," said Bernard grimly.

Rosalind's little intake of breath was audible. She realized now, for the first time, to what an extent one part of herself had been holding aloof from the reality of the situation at Bell House. For all the series of emotions she had experienced that afternoon, there had remained this hard core in her that had been looking on, as if at a drama on the stage. But with this brief remark of Bernard's all illusion fled. At the same time she suddenly recollected what it was that had been hovering at the back of her mind when Garry had told them he'd discovered the loss of the plants about half an hour previously.

"Enough to kill a human being?" she asked Bernard.

"In the case of the hemlock water dropwort, the answer is quite probably yes," he replied. "People have died from eating a couple of leaves in mistake for celery. There were many more than a couple of leaves on the piece I picked for you. Not to mention the juice from the stems. That's the one I'm really worried about. There'd be no need to go out and pick some more in that case."

Rosalind slid down into the chair on whose arm she was perched and leaned back against the cushion. The shock of her own recollection had made her feel physically weak.

"I haven't taken those plants, Bernard," she said after a moment's pause. "I haven't got them."

"I never supposed you had."

"But—" She stopped and swallowed convulsively. "What do you want me to do?" she asked after another pause.

"Nothing. Just try to believe in me."

"I—" Rosalind was finding it very difficult to talk. To be like Garry, she thought; to be like this all the time, not just momentarily . . . why, one would be constantly feeling like a volcano unable to explode. "I don't think we'd better talk about those plant specimens any more," she said at last. "It's all speculation. I don't think it would be helpful to go on about it."

"Neither do I. But you did ask me."

"And you did explain to the whole lot of us the properties of the poisonous plants, and they were labelled, so that anyone who was not able to identify them before could easily do so now." Rosalind passed a hand across her eyes. "This is a nightmare," she said in a muffled voice. "Surely we must wake up soon."

"It's the sort of nightmare I've been living with for years," said Bernard. "Jane's tried this on me before, you know. But I've coped with it without dragging anyone else in. And now I have gone and dragged in somebody else and of all people it has to be the one woman in the world whom I feel I could—"

"Don't start that again," interrupted Rosalind. "You're not responsible for my actions. I'm a free agent. We're both free agents. We have to act independently."

"I'm afraid we do. I wish we could pool our suspicions, but I see you would prefer not to and I quite understand."

"Thanks," said Rosalind. She got up and held on to the back of the chair. "I think I'd better go. I promised Martin I'd try to be home within the hour."

"Have you changed your mind about leaving Swallow-fields?" asked Bernard as they came out on to the lawn.

"I think I'd better stay here for the time being," said Rosalind. "At least until this business is cleared up."

"What makes you think it is going to be 'cleared up,' as you call it?"

"It must be! We've got to find out who took those plants, at any rate," cried Rosalind in desperation.

"Suppose nobody admits to it?"

"But they must! We can't all go on living in this ghastly welter of suspicion. It's unbearable."

"You ought to know how long people can live in unbearable situations," said Bernard.

They had reached the house. Without saying another word Rosalind collected her handbag that she had left on a chair in the big sitting-room and ran out of the front door. The gravel of the front drive slowed her down. She had put on some white summer shoes in honour of the invitation to Bell House and their heels were higher than she was accustomed to wearing. Near the open gates of the drive she stumbled on a stone as she ran, and she put out a hand to the gatepost to steady herself for a moment before taking a few steps along by the beech hedge that separated the front garden from the lane. When she judged herself to be out of sight of the house she bent down to remove a piece of gravel that had lodged itself under the strap of one of her sandals. She felt sure that Bernard had been standing on the front doorstep of Bell House, watching her run awkwardly down the drive, and she was afraid that if she appeared to be in any discomfort, he would use it as an excuse to come after her.

Rosalind wriggled her toes in relief and was just about to straighten up again when her eye was caught by what looked like a tiny scrap of paper lying in the grass between the beech hedge and the lane. The hedge itself was well trimmed but the grass verge had got rather out of control at a time of year when all green things were growing at a pace almost visible to the naked eye. Rosalind, who hated litter in the streets and public places, reached out for the scrap of paper more with the intention of removing it from an otherwise unlittered grass bank than from any motive of curiosity. It was only when she found that in picking up the piece of paper she was also picking up some of the greenery around, that her mind began its relentless reasoning.

For the paper was in fact a small card label with writing on it, and it was attached by means of a narrow strip of adhesive tape to the stem of a plant. Above the tape the stem branched into pretty feathery leaves and further up still it narrowed and looked as if something had been broken off, perhaps a flower. Rosalind glanced round to make sure that there was nobody in sight in the lane and that she was well concealed from the house by the high beech hedge, and then she looked closely at the label. She recognized the clear but immature writing immediately. It was Garry's.

"*Oenanthe phellandrium*," she read. "Water Fennel or Water Dropwort. Flower rather inadequate as it does not normally bloom till July."

A great surge of relief went through her as she read. That's the one, she said to herself. That's the Latin name—*Oenanthe*. That's the one he said was the real killer. Martin must have dropped it without noticing when he pulled out the plants that he had been hiding under his loose shirt. They must have tickled him terribly and he would have pulled them out to carry in his hand the moment he was out of sight of the house. But he would have been in a great hurry. It would have been only too easy for one of them to fall to the ground unseen.

Had he dropped any of the others in his haste?

Rosalind laid her white handbag on the grass and placed the labelled specimen carefully on top of it. Then she began to search the area on hands and knees, frequently looking up to check that she was not being observed. She was rewarded by finding two more items tucked away under the hedge, so deep in the surrounding green growth that the labels would not have been visible had she not been very carefully searching. As indeed the first specimen would not have caught her eye had she not been bending down to attend to her shoe.

Rosalind squatted back on her heels in the long grass and examined her finds. The labels of both were still sticking to the stems, but one of them she did not even trouble to read. Here was Bernard's "particularly nice little foxglove," squashed and with the top broken off, but unmistakable. The other plant, also very squashed, was an indeterminate-looking piece of green-ery, but Rosalind did not read further than *Daucus carota*. Carrot, she said to herself: that would be another of the harmless ones. He would have thrown this away on purpose, together with the other innocent plant, whose name she could not at the moment remember. She debated for a moment or two whether to search further, trying to recreate Martin's state of mind as he left Bell House.

It was the way he had been scratching at himself during those moments when they stood talking in the garden that had given her the clue. At the time she had genuinely thought Martin had been suffering from the irritating nervous skin trouble that affected him from time to time, and later the impression had faded from her mind so that when she tried to recall it she had been unable to. It was not until her final talk with Bernard that the revelation had come and the theft of the plant specimens and Martin's behaviour had slipped into place. His questions about how much longer she intended to stay at Bell House that afternoon also fitted in. Rosalind had thought at the time that he resented her staying on and wanted her to come home with him, but the frightening light of revelation showed that he had a very different motive: he wanted to go home and be sure of having the cottage to himself for a while before she turned up herself. And he wanted to be alone so that he could experiment with the specimens he had stolen from the refrigerator in the stillroom.

Or at any rate, with some of them. It was possible, thought Rosalind, that Martin had actually thrown away the harmless plants before he had talked to her on the lawn. He could have come round to the front of the house pretending to look for Garry, gone just outside the gate, and dropped the unnecessary plants in the hedge, leaving only one or two concealed under his shirt when she met him. Which ones would those be?

There had been six specimens in all. Three were now accounted for. The foxglove, which though poisonous was unlikely to attract Martin as an object for experiment; the harmless wild carrot; and the one that Bernard had said was the real killer and which Martin must surely have dropped by mistake. That left three more, two of which would be harmless and one of which would be hemlock. Real hemlock, deadly enough but with a smell and a taste that nobody could possibly mistake. Martin would have taken that home with him, and the other two harmless plants were probably lying under the hedge somewhere.

Rosalind decided that she would not bother to look any further. What Martin's motives were she did not at the moment want to know, nor did she yet know whether she was going to challenge him with stealing the plants. The whole business was horrible enough, but it might have been even worse. Whether he had succeeded in extracting the juice from the hemlock specimen, or whether he was simply keeping it with a view to using it for identification when he went out to look for some more, Rosalind did not at the moment care. All that concerned her was that by great good fortune he had gone and lost the real killer.

She picked up her handbag and the first of the labelled sprays that she had found and glanced at it again. The leaves really were very delicate and pretty, rather like a fern. Even as this comparison occurred to her another comparison flashed into her mind. Something Bernard had said. People have died from eating the leaves in mistake for celery.

Celery? Surely nobody could mistake these leaves for celery? With a sudden surge of misgiving, Rosalind read the label again.

"Water Fennel or Water Dropwort . . ."

Wasn't that the one Bernard had called the most poisonous of the lot? The Latin was the same, and surely the English name had been Water Dropwort?

It had. But there had been hemlock in the name too. Hemlock Water Dropwort. And the *Oenanthe* had been followed by a different Latin word from that on the card. In other words, thought Rosalind, walking along the lane as quickly as her shoes would allow, she had mixed up the very similar names of two different plants in her mind, and the one she was holding was a harmless, or comparatively harmless, cousin of the dangerous one that Martin had no doubt taken home with him.

It was impossible to avoid thinking about Martin's motives now. It was also impossible to believe that Martin was capable of poisoning anybody or of taking any action that could lead to a false accusation of attempted poisoning by someone else. Of

course he had many faults. Rosalind tried to assess her
son's character in a dispassionate way as she hurried along the
country road, quite unaware of the beauty of the mild June
evening. He had bad moods and fits of sulks and fury. He was
terribly possessive and jealous about herself, terribly touchy
about his father. In fact he was given to extreme emotions of all
kinds, chivalrous and quixotic feelings as well as aggressive
feelings.

That was Martin. But the same could also be said of
countless youngsters of Martin's age and very few of them did
any permanent harm to anybody. Some of them did drastic and
silly things, though. Like suicide attempts, for example. But
surely that could be ruled out in Martin's case. He had bad fits
of depression, but he had come through the horror of his
father's death and his mother's arrest with astonishing forti-
tude. And the present situation, however distressing for him,
was nothing like so great an ordeal.

On the other hand he had certainly taken those poisonous
plants, and Rosalind could not believe that he intended to use
them for a purely scientific experiment. If that had been the
case he would have talked about it openly. There would not
have been that furious reaction when she found he was reading
about how Socrates died after drinking the hemlock, nor the
hiding of the plant specimens and the great anxiety to have her
out of the cottage for a while.

So engrossed was Rosalind in her anxious speculations that
she barely noticed that she had turned the corner from the quiet
lane into the busier road that led to Swallowfields. She walked
on the grass verge and was unaware of the passing cars until
one actually drew up alongside and hooted. Rosalind looked up
to see a red Mini with two of its wheels on the grass. The driver
was leaning across and opening the passenger door. She was a
pretty dark-haired girl with a worried expression on her face.

"Isn't Martin with you?" she asked.

"Hullo, Deirdre. No, I'm afraid he isn't," said Rosalind.
"He went home about an hour ago." She got into the car. She
had not realized how exhausted she was until she sat down.
"Isn't he at home now?" she asked.

"No. Or rather, I don't know."

"How d'you mean, you don't know?"

"I've been ringing the bell and knocking for ages," replied Deirdre, "and there's no reply. But I've got a sort of feeling he's in the house and doesn't want to let me in. I know it sounds silly," she added apologetically, "but that's how it felt, and I can't help being worried. You don't think he's getting tired of me, do you, Rosalind, and this is his way of telling me to push off?"

At the sound of the anxious young voice Rosalind came fully back to herself and took a decision.

"I'm sure he's not getting tired of you, Deirdre," she said with as much warmth of reassurance as she could muster, "but he's in a very odd mood, as you know, and this afternoon there were all sorts of things happening at the Goodwins' house. If you'll turn round and drive slowly back to Swallowfields I'll tell you as quickly as I can."

12

Rosalind was only half way through her story by the end of the short drive back. Deirdre turned the Mini into the entrance of the church and they sat there looking across the road at the cottage while Rosalind finished.

"What do you want me to do?" asked the girl. She sounded worried but determined, as she had been when she put her arms round Rosalind in the cottage kitchen and promised her that everything would come all right, and Rosalind felt sure that she had done the right thing in telling Deirdre everything without reserve.

"Try and find out what he's up to," she replied. "You can do it much better than I can. Martin and I can no longer talk to each other. But of course, not to let on that you know anything about what I've just been saying. As if you needed telling that!"

"Right," said Deirdre. "Then we'd better not arrive together. I hope he's not seen us from a window."

"There's only my bedroom window this side," said Rosalind. "I think we're all right. I'll go first since I've got the key. You come in about five minutes as if you'd just arrived."

She opened the passenger door.

"Just a minute," said Deirdre, touching her arm. "What are we going to do about those plants?"

Rosalind looked down at the three rapidly withering specimens that she still held in her hand. "I'd better not let him

know I found them till we know how the land lies," she said.
"But I don't want to lose them. They could be important
evidence if it ever came to . . ."

Her voice faded away. Confiding in Deirdre had given her a
great renewal of strength, but she still could not bear to think
what "it" might come to.

"Leave them in the car," said Deirdre. "I'll hang on to
them."

"They're getting a bit battered. They'll be unrecognizable
soon, but I daren't bring any water out in case Martin sees me."

"I'm going into the churchyard," said Deirdre with great
determination, "and I'll pinch a vase off one of the graves and
put these in it and leave it on the floor at the back of the car."

"You bad girl," said Rosalind, smiling as she opened the
door. "Turning criminal like the rest of us!"

"Dad will always bail me out," said Deirdre quite seriously.
"And Martin too if need be."

"Let's hope it won't come to that," said Rosalind, her smile
fading.

When she reached the front gate of the cottage she heard a
familiar voice utter a friendly greeting.

"Nice evening, Mrs. Bannister."

It was PC Arthur Bancroft, resident in the village at the
police house a little way up Church Lane. He was large, solid
and middle-aged, and had kept a fatherly eye on Swallowfields
and its neighbouring hamlets for the past ten years. Very little
that went on in the area escaped Arthur. He chatted freely to
everybody, but could be discretion itself when necessary, and
had been known to turn a blind eye to minor misdemeanours if
he felt that to prosecute would mean endangering the peace and
good feeling of the community. He knew Rosalind's own
history and she sometimes felt that he had a soft spot for her
because of it and that in some subtle way impossible to pin
down, PC Arthur Bancroft had helped her to be accepted and
become part of the village life. Normally she was always
pleased to see him, but at this moment she wished him
anywhere except at her own front gate.

"Hullo, Arthur," she replied as brightly as she could.
"Everyone behaving themselves today?"

"No great villainies so far," he replied. "Fine weather makes for good tempers and good tempers make for peaceable people. Little outbreak of pot plants, that's all."

"Pot plants?" echoed Rosalind blankly, glancing across the front yard to see whether she could see Martin at the kitchen window. There was no sign of him and she could not see further into the room from where she stood.

"Marijuana," said Arthur. "We get an outbreak of it now and then. Usually among the young folk. Those with enquiring minds and a scientific bent, you might say. This one had never tried it before so I've just left him a warning. I doubt if he'll do it again. Never had any trouble that way with your lad, I suppose?"

It was said with the friendliest of intentions, Rosalind had no doubt. Martin clearly fell within the category of youngsters who might be at risk in this respect. A few days ago Rosalind would have taken Arthur's remark entirely in the spirit in which it was offered and would have promised him to keep a look-out and stamp on any such experiments at once. But now she hardly knew how to compose herself for a suitable reply. Marijuana, cannabis, pot—whatever you liked to call it, it seemed so irrelevant and so harmless in comparison with the experiments with plants that she suspected Martin of conducting.

"Martin's never shown any tendency that way," she said, trying to sound mildly amused but knowing she was not succeeding. "In fact I can't get him to take any interest in any sort of gardening at all."

"Pity," said Arthur. "You could do with a bit of help with the heavier jobs now and then. I'll send one of my boys along to lend you a hand if ever you need it. Don't forget now."

Rosalind thanked him.

"That's all right then. Any time you need help. See you at the committee meeting tomorrow?"

"Oh yes. Of course. Goodbye for now."

Rosalind had completely forgotten the meeting, although up till a few days ago she had looked forward to it as one of the high spots in her quiet life. The meetings of the village hall committee, of which Arthur had been secretary for years and on to which Rosalind had recently been co-opted, were held at the house of the chairman, Lesley Green, and they were pleasant social occasions in addition to being very business-like.

Arthur turned away and Rosalind put her key in the door. "Hullo, darling," she called loudly as she came into the hall, deliberately making more noise than was necessary so that Martin could have no excuse for saying that she was creeping into the cottage and spying on him.

These precautions turned out to be unnecessary.

"Hello, Mum," called out Martin in a normal-sounding voice. "I've had my supper."

He was sitting at the kitchen table drinking coffee and reading the local weekly paper. A plate that looked as if it had contained something soaked in tomato sauce was pushed to one side.

"Saw you being accosted by the fuzz," he said. "Let you off with a warning this time?"

Now that she had come closer to him Rosalind could sense the strain under Martin's attempts to patch up their relationship.

"We have been warned," she said as lightly as she could, "not to try to grow marijuana."

"Marijuana?" Martin spoke as if he had never heard the word before.

"Apparently there is a little outbreak of it in the village."

Martin laughed and took a drink of coffee. "That's it, that's the answer," he cried as he put his cup down. "All that stillroom stage-set. It's window-dressing. Obviously Bernard Goodwin is running a drug racket from Bell House. Or Garry's running it for him. And Bernard's got some hold over him. And in any case Garry can't talk."

"Nonsense," said Rosalind sharply. "There was no sign of any marijuana up there."

"How do you know? Would you recognize it if you saw it?"

"Yes," said Rosalind firmly and untruthfully. "And in any case, if something like that was going on, you could be quite sure Arthur would know about it. He knows everything that goes on in Swallowfields."

"Bell House isn't Swallowfields," said Martin. "They've managed to keep themselves to themselves. We didn't even know Garry existed till this afternoon, and no one knew anything about Jane."

This was very true. The Goodwins had definitely not been part of village society. But today had brought an end to their isolation, thought Rosalind, and it was definitely Bernard's own doing. He seemed to have reached some sort of crisis in his own life and she, Rosalind, was part of it. The notions that she was trying hard to repress broke through to the surface yet again. Bernard was beginning to feel about her as she felt about him, and Jane, who up till now had been simply a tiresome burden, was now an obstacle in the way of his own happiness. Could Garry and Martin and Jane herself be right after all? Was Bernard really capable of poisoning Jane?

"All the same," said Rosalind firmly to Martin, "I'm sure he's not growing pot up there. It's not worth risking his whole career."

Martin drained his coffee-cup before replying. Then he said: "You're probably right. He's not interested in anything as harmless as marijuana."

Rosalind bit back a sharp retort. It seemed that there was only to be a truce, not a complete reconciliation, between herself and her son. Nevertheless it would be best to make the truce last as long as possible, in fairness to Deirdre if for no other reason. Rosalind had assured the girl that Martin's quixotic reaction to Jane was no threat to the young people's friendship, but obviously Deirdre would be anxious until she saw Martin for herself.

"Had enough to eat?" Rosalind asked instead. "D'you want me to get you anything more?"

"No, thanks. I've taken the last tin of baked beans, by the way."

"I'll get some more tomorrow. What shall I have myself?" Rosalind glanced round the kitchen. "I don't feel exactly hungry but I feel I'd like something."

"Why don't you fall back on eggs?" suggested Martin. This was an old joke between them and it showed that his good humour still held.

"I suppose I could," said Rosalind without much enthusiasm, and wishing Deirdre would hurry up and come. She moved across to the sink and took a bowl down from the cupboard above. It was at that moment that she first noticed what was standing in the plate rack on the draining-board, and the words shot out of her before she could stop them.

"Good heavens, isn't that the juice separator attachment for the foodmixer? Don't tell me you've actually managed to find out how it works!"

She had won the gadget in a raffle a few weeks previously, and not being a particularly keen or adventurous cook, had not yet troubled to make use of it. Martin had expressed some interest in it at the time and had said it looked rather complicated but he would try to get it working one of these days, and they had agreed that it would be rather nice to have fresh fruit and vegetable juice during the summer.

"Tried it on an orange," said Martin, picking up the paper again. "It's not all that difficult. I'll show you some time."

Rosalind made no reply. An orange, she said to herself as she switched on the kettle to make herself coffee; I suppose it's just possible that that is true. She glanced at Martin. He was studying the paper with an air of intense concentration. No, of course it's not true, she thought suddenly. You don't use the juice separator to get orange juice. You use the other gadget— the juice extractor for citrus fruit.

Martin turned a page of the paper and Rosalind's thoughts raced on. The silence between them became unbearable. At last there came the ring at the door. "I'll go," said Rosalind and rushed out of the kitchen.

"Hullo, Deirdre," she called out a moment later with what she hoped sounded like surprise. "Are we expecting you? Martin's had his meal but if you'd like to join me in something . . ."

"Hullo, infant." Martin had reached the front door so quickly that Rosalind was glad she had not attempted to convey any private message to Deirdre by look or by gesture.

"Hullo, Martin," said the girl. "I wondered if you felt like a drive or a walk or a bit of practising or something."

Martin gave this his consideration. "Not a walk or a drive,

I think," he said at last. "Nor do I feel in the right mood for trying to play Haydn. But I'll hear your solo bit in the Bartók if you've got your fiddle in the car. Let's go and fetch it."

The plants, thought Rosalind with alarm, trying and failing to think up a reason why Martin should not accompany Deirdre to the Mini. It was not until the two young people returned a few minutes later, chatting together quite happily, that Rosalind realized that Deirdre must have thought of this herself or she would not have suggested Martin coming for a drive.

She made herself some coffee and sat at the kitchen table, looking out across the courtyard at the gradually lengthening shadows in the village street. Everything looked and felt perfectly normal, both outside the cottage and within. There had been many such evenings since Martin had first brought Deirdre to see her six months ago. Rosalind tried hard to believe that it was possible for them all to return to what in retrospect had been a happy state, although at the time it had been for herself a sort of dim half-existence, lightened only by the satisfaction of seeing Martin happy in the company of this delightful warm-hearted girl.

It was no good. She could not even sincerely wish to return to that state. It was not in her nature to live entirely through her son. Even if they were to leave the village and she were never to see Bernard again, there could be no going back because the change was in herself. If Martin could not accept it then the outlook was bleak for him as well as for her. And she could not help him. Deirdre was her only hope.

Rosalind got up from the table and took her coffee cup over to the sink to rinse it under the tap. After she had turned it upside down to drain she did what she had been pretending to herself that she was not going to do: picked up the various parts of the juice separator and examined them closely. Martin's washing up was always rather hasty and careless, and it was just possible that a tell-tale fragment might still be clinging to one of the plastic or metal pieces.

Finding no sign of either green fragments or of orange fragments, Rosalind looked next at the wooden bowl that stood in its usual place on the wide window-sill of the kitchen. It contained three apples and two oranges. Rosalind shut her eyes for a moment in order to regain a mental image of the kitchen as it had been before they set out to visit the Goodwins at Bell House. There had been three oranges in the bowl: she was quite sure of that. So Martin had taken an orange. There was no sign of any peel on the table or the draining-board and Rosalind raised the lid of the pedal-bin that stood near the sink with a feeling of excitement that she was getting somewhere at last, combined with distaste with herself for spying on her son. She had emptied the bin herself that morning, and there would be very little in it except what Martin had put there.

Rosalind bent closer. The empty baked bean tin caught her eye at once. Next to it lay some screwed up pieces of kitchen paper, and sticking out from underneath one of them she could see a piece of orange peel. She put a hand into the bin and pushed the paper aside: more orange peel came into view. Rosalind knelt down on the floor and held up the lid with her hand while she studied the contents of the bin, thinking so intently that she forgot to listen for any sign of movement on the floor above or on the stairs of the cottage.

The peel proved that Martin had taken an orange, as he had said, but could it possibly be true that he had put the peeled orange through the juice separator? He was much better than she was at following instructions and he would have seen at once that this was not the right way to extract orange juice. Whether or not he expected her to believe him Rosalind could not guess. He might think her too stupid to realize the difference between the two types of juice equipment, or he might be so sure that he had left no other clue that he did not care whether she suspected him or not.

Was there really no other clue? What about the pieces of kitchen paper? Rosalind pulled them out of the bin and, still squatting on the floor, uncrumpled each piece in turn. They were damp, as if they had been used as a wiping-up cloth, and two of them had smudges of an indeterminate colour—green, brown, yellow—it seemed to be a mixture of all three. A phrase from Bernard's informal lecture in the stillroom that afternoon came into Rosalind's mind: The stems of the plant contain a yellow juice that is not unpleasant to the taste.

Rosalind crushed the pieces of flimsy paper together in her

right hand and let fall the lid of the pedal-bin. This was more like real evidence. These stains could be analysed. If they turned out to have come from the stem of that poisonous plant, the likelihood would be that Martin had indeed managed to extract its juice and had used the kitchen paper to wipe the parts of the machine.

Firm evidence. But did she really want to hold on to this evidence against her own son? Suppose there were to be a poisoning or an attempted poisoning. Was she going to come forward to the police with the pieces of paper and her theory of what Martin had been doing? What sort of a mother was that, who could spy on and help condemn her own child?

In a fit of horrified revulsion Rosalind lifted the lid of the pedal-bin and dropped the ball of paper on top of the baked bean tin. Then she snatched it back again. I'm never actually going to use it, she told herself; I'm just going to keep it somewhere safe in case. But where? And where was Martin keeping that little bit of deadly liquid that she now felt quite sure he possessed? It was unthinkable that they should continue to live together in this cottage, each with such a secret to hide from the other.

Such were Rosalind's thoughts when she heard the quick footstep on the stairs. There was no time to scramble to her feet and put the pedal-bin back in its usual place, so she remained where she was, telling herself fatalistically that it was bound to blow up some time between Martin and herself and it might be as well to get it over.

— 13 —

"Rosalind! Are you all right?"

The sound of Deirdre's voice came almost as a disappointment. Rosalind got up in a dazed manner, still clutching the screwed-up paper, and unable to think of any reason to give Deirdre why she had been sitting on the floor.

The girl did not notice that the pedal-bin was out of place. "You gave me quite a fright," she went on. "I thought you'd had a heart attack or something."

She closed the kitchen door behind her and continued in a low voice: "I'm afraid I haven't got anything out of him but he seems to be quite cheerful. I told him I'd come down to get myself some coffee? May I?"

"Of course."

"You don't think," went on Deirdre as she switched on the kettle, "that it could have been somebody else who took those plants? The dumb boy, perhaps?"

She looked at Rosalind appealingly, obviously longing to believe that their suspicions of Martin were unfounded. She's a good girl and a strong girl, thought Rosalind, but she's very young. She's ready to take on Martin's jealousy and resentment and moodiness, but she can't really face the possibility that he could do anything criminal. Rosalind made a sudden decision. It had not been quite fair to burden Deirdre with her suspicions of Martin: it put the girl into an impossible position with him. If anyone were to lose Martin, it must be Rosalind herself, not this girl who so clearly loved him and who had her whole life ahead of her.

"As a matter of fact," she said firmly, "I'd just come to that conclusion myself. When you came in I was just checking something that quite convinced me Martin had nothing to do with it."

"Oh Rosalind!" Deirdre looked up from pouring water on the coffee powder. "I'm so relieved, you can't imagine. Not that I ever really thought Martin could ever . . . but he does get very worked up sometimes . . ."

"I think you'd better throw away those plants I gave you," said Rosalind.

"Oh, but mightn't they still be needed as evidence? Against that poor boy, I mean. I'm sure Dad would say they ought to be kept. I've locked them in the boot, by the way. In the vase I got off a grave. I'll bring it back tomorrow."

"I leave it to you," replied Rosalind. "I can't argue with a lawyer's daughter. Are you going to tell your father about all this, by the way?"

"Well, I would rather like to tell him about the plants being missing and you finding some of them, but I won't say anything much about Martin. And I won't mention that other boy either. It wouldn't be fair, since we don't really know anything, do we?"

"No, we don't really know anything," agreed Rosalind.

"And we don't really know that anything awful is going to happen either," said Deirdre.

"We don't indeed. Let's hope it won't."

"I'm *sure* it won't." Deirdre flung her arms around Rosalind for a moment and then picked up her coffee-cup. "Please try not to worry, darling Rosalind," she said. "I'm sure it will all turn out all right."

After Deirdre had left the kitchen Rosalind replaced the pedal-bin in its usual position and looked around for a suitable hiding-place for the ball of kitchen paper. In the end she went into her little scullery studio and pushed it into a drawer containing rags and pieces of scrap paper and similar odds and ends. It was hardly likely that Martin would search there, or indeed anywhere else, for something that he had carelessly thrown into the rubbish bin. In fact the more she thought about this carelessness, the more did Rosalind feel how unlikely it was that Martin had any serious intention of making use of the poisonous juice. On the other hand, was it after all so very careless? If she had not found those plant specimens in the long grass near the entrance to Bell House she would not have been so sure that Martin had taken them, and it had been pure chance that she had found them there.

Rosalind's thoughts went round and round, finding no resting-place. Doubts about Martin were succeeded by doubts about Bernard, which were followed in turn by long speculations as to what, if anything, she herself could do to prevent tragedy. In the midst of all this she would suddenly say to herself, as firmly as Deirdre had said, that it was all going to turn out all right. But the next moment she would be on the treadmill again. In an attempt to find relief she sat down at her drawing-board and made a few desultory pencil strokes on a fresh sheet of paper. The pencil was dead between her fingers. There was nothing of the familiar little thrill of starting on a new design, however humble or trivial the product on which it was to be used. All delight in her own skill had deserted her and she felt that it would never return unless she could share it with another. She put down the pencil and propped her chin on her hands. There was no point in pretending to herself any longer. For the second time in her life she had fallen deeply in love. She wanted to share her gifts and all that was in her with Bernard. Life held no meaning otherwise. Whatever evil he might have done was forgiven in advance. It made no difference to her feelings. And at last fully facing the truth, she knew what she was going to do. If Bernard were in any danger from Martin, then she must protect him, even at the cost of grievously hurting her son. Martin must come second. It was a terrible decision to take, but when it was taken the strength and resolution began at once to flow back.

The music stopped on the floor above and there were sounds of footsteps. Rosalind hurriedly picked up her pencil again, and when Deirdre came into the kitchen she was drawing little decorative leaves all round the edge of the paper.

"That's pretty," said the girl standing in the doorway to the scullery. "What's it going to be?"

"Nothing in particular." Rosalind looked up with a smile. "I'm just doodling."

The girl seemed remote to her. It was as if with her decision she had jumped a chasm and Deirdre and Martin were the other side.

"I wish my doodles looked like that," said Deirdre.

"I wish I could play the violin like you," retorted Rosalind.

"Martin's cheered up no end," said Deirdre, obviously getting round to what she really wanted to say now the polite preliminaries were over. "He says he would like to come out for a drive after all. We'll probably be quite late. We're going to go down to the coast and look at the moonlight over the sea."

"How very romantic," said Rosalind, and was afraid the moment she had spoken that it sounded rather sarcastic and not just rather amused, as she had intended. But Deirdre was not listening, because Martin had come into the kitchen and was asking her if she wanted a midnight swim. Deirdre replied that it was too cold; Martin called her a coward, and they went off together bickering affectionately. On the surface they appeared to be quite back to normal, but Rosalind could not help wondering what Martin had said in reply to Deirdre's no doubt tactful enquiries about the stolen plants. She was reluctant to believe that Martin would deliberately accuse Garry, and in the end she decided that he had probably given Deirdre a flat denial which the girl was only too happy to believe. That it was the happiness of illusion Rosalind had no doubt. Martin was not only lying to the girl about the plants, but also keeping quiet about the attraction that Jane Goodwin had for him. But at any rate the young people's moonlight jaunt gave Rosalind the chance she wanted to have a thorough look round Martin's room, and as soon as she had seen the Mini disappear round the bend in the road beyond the church, she ran upstairs and began a systematic search of Martin's possessions.

His room was the larger of the two attic bedrooms on the upper floor of the cottage and it was crammed tight with things. Martin was a hoarder, and a very untidy one, and the whole history of his short life could be read in the muddle in his room. Babyhood was there in the battered Teddy-bear and stuffed dog that he refused to part with. Childhood had its quota of model cars and aeroplanes, toy soldiers and similar items now untouched and gathering dust on the shelves. Then came the remains of the period when he was going to be an architect— piles of designs for buildings of various sorts, the paper now dog-eared and crumpled, and a half-completed model for a community centre that was to fulfil some glorious adolescent dream of how human beings ought to live together and help each other. This was followed by the interest in science which had persisted to the present moment and looked like determining Martin's future career.

Fortunately, thought Rosalind as she carefully examined the contraptions that Martin had set up on top of the chest of drawers and on the broad window-sill, it had never been directed towards biology or zoology, and she had been spared spiders in bottles and cardboard boxes containing revolting-looking parts of animals, or even—horror of horrors—snakes in the bath. Chemistry had been the worst, with the messes and smells in the kitchen and the constant apprehension that something was going to explode, but on the whole Martin's experimenting had been to do with weight and mass and force and had involved comparatively inoffensive pieces of apparatus that looked like egg-timers, weighing scales, or the works of clocks, and that didn't stink or look as if they might go off with a bang even if they did collapse or go wrong.

Music had been the last arrival among his enthusiasms and the violin was better cared for than the majority of his belongings, partly owing to Rosalind's threat that she was never going to buy him another if he broke it, and partly, no doubt, owing to the influence of his fellow music-lover, Deirdre.

The books on the shelves revealed the same progression of a boy's mind. So did the pictures and the posters on the walls. Had Rosalind been in a nostalgic or reminiscent frame of mind she could have lingered grievingly over every item. But she never allowed herself such sentiments and in any case she was thoroughly familiar with all Martin's possessions from her attempts to keep down the worst of the dust. She could see almost at a glance which places had been recently in use and which had not. The latter were quickly disposed of, leaving her free to concentrate on the contents of the table and the wardrobe.

Rosalind tackled the table first. She was determined not to be found in Martin's room and was constantly alert to any sign that the youngsters were returning unexpectedly early. But if by evil chance she was caught in there, she would prefer Martin to find her looking among his clothes rather than among the muddle on the table. Obviously he would not believe any excuse she made, but if she said she had come to fetch his jacket to mend the pocket he would find it very hard to disprove her.

It was therefore with some relief that Rosalind transferred her search to the contents of the wardrobe. Martin did not possess many clothes compared with many of his generation, and it didn't take long to feel in all the pockets and in the lining where a pocket had torn and an object could slip through. When she had finished this part of the operation she paused for a moment, thinking.

What was it that she was looking for? Some small bottle, like those standing on the table either empty or containing what looked like salt. A very tiny bottle that would contain a tiny quantity of a liquid—a yellow liquid, Bernard had said. But she was not going to find it, because Martin would have kept this deadly juice on him. Even he was not going to be so careless as to leave it somewhere where his mother could come across it by chance. He might have got it in his jeans or in one of the zip-up pockets of the anorak Rosalind had noticed he was wearing when he and Deirdre left the house. He was not really intending to bathe, she thought; he would never leave his clothes unattended.

The sound of a car drawing up just outside the cottage at this moment sent Rosalind rushing into her own bedroom to look out of the window. It was Lesley Green's little Fiat, and a moment later there was both a knock and a ring at the door. Rosalind remained upstairs, feeling guilty but determined not to answer. It was growing dark now, and there was no light shining from the cottage. A minute or two later the car drove off and Rosalind came downstairs to find that an envelope had been pushed through the letter-box. She picked it up and went into the living-room and sat down in her usual chair beside the fireplace and switched on the reading-lamp.

The envelope contained papers to be considered at the forthcoming committee meeting. Rosalind tried to read them but found her mind kept wandering back to Martin. If he had managed to extract some juice and had it on him, that would still leave the pulp of one or two plants and also the labels unaccounted for. Presumably the pulp had been washed down the sink. The machine would have ensured that it would be fine enough to be so disposed of, and nothing remained but the stains on the kitchen paper. Had the labels been similarly pulped?

Rosalind looked up from the estimates for an extension to the village hall and stared at the empty grate. There were several cigarette stubs lying there. Both she and Martin smoked in moderation and both of them had a habit of using the open fireplace as an ashtray, winter and summer alike, when they were sitting in this room. Mucky habit, thought Rosalind, and I never swept out the grate this morning.

She knelt down, picked up the hearthbrush, and swept the cigarette ends into her cupped hand. A little black ash came along with them and all the mechanism of suspicion in her mind began to hum again.

It wasn't ash left over from last winter's fires. Nor was it soot. It was quite fresh; the sort of deposit left from burning paper. She brushed a little harder and found what looked like a scrap of unburnt card. She put down the brush, licked a finger, and let the scrap stick to it. As far as she could see it contained no ink mark. But he's not to know that, she said to herself. He can't be sure. If he burnt the labels there could easily be a little of the writing still left on an unburnt bit of paper. It's the sort of thing nobody would ever notice unless they were specifically looking for it. It won't be hard to fake something and pretend I found it here while cleaning out the grate. If I challenge him with it perhaps I'll get the truth out of him.

For a long time Rosalind knelt in front of the empty grate, the cigarette ends held in her left hand and the scrap of paper stuck to the forefinger of her right. The thought of playing a trick like that on her son horrified her. But the thought of taking no action at all horrified her even more.

14

"But you must come to the meeting this evening!" cried Lesley Green over the telephone the following morning. "Mr. Goodwin has promised to come along, just as an observer, but we're hoping he might allow himself to be co-opted on to the committee."

"When did you invite him?" asked Rosalind.

"On the phone—just before I rang you. He was just going up to London. He made polite remarks about my elderberry wine and promised to look in this evening on his way home. Quite a triumph, isn't it, to get him. Mind you, I'm under no illusions about the reasons for his accepting."

"What d'you mean?" asked Rosalind with a little quickening of the heartbeat because she had guessed what her friend was going to say next.

"He's coming because you'll be there of course," was the uncompromising reply. "He asked me who was on the committee and didn't show any reaction when I ran through the names until I mentioned yours and then there was a distinct change of gear. So you see, Ros, you've simply got to come. You've made a hit there, my girl."

"I sincerely hope not," said Rosalind, feeling anything but sincere as she spoke. "Mr. Goodwin has got a wife. You've not said this to anyone else, I hope, Lesley?" she added anxiously. "I mean, the very last thing I need, even in fun—"

"Have you ever known me to gossip?" demanded the voice at the other end of the line.

"Sorry," said Rosalind. "Shows I'm a bit off colour, taking that sort of remark seriously. I don't feel very well. Honestly. Seem to have eaten something that disagreed with me."

"Bad luck, old thing. Did they give you some herbal concoction up at Bell House?"

Rosalind tried to laugh. "Oh no. It was a perfectly civilized occasion. It wasn't till this morning that I started feeling rotten."

"Delayed action. Oh well, if you're really ill, I suppose there's no more to be said. Anyway, you've served your purpose, my dear. He thinks you're going to be there so he's coming."

There were times when Rosalind felt she could do without the bluntness on which Lesley Green prided herself. This was one of those times. She tried very hard to keep a certain warmth of friendship in her voice as she repeated that she didn't feel well at the moment but would come if she felt better by the evening. Lesley softened enough to ask if Rosalind needed any errands done, and when this offer was politely rejected the conversation came to an end. Rosalind put the receiver back with the feeling that this little talk had made an already bad situation even worse. Lesley probably would not say anything deliberately, because she was fond of Rosalind and was fundamentally honest and good-hearted; nevertheless, it would soon be all round the village that Bernard Goodwin, that delightful man with an unsatisfactory wife, was very interested in Rosalind Bannister, the quiet woman with a past. Still waters run deep, they would say, and how they would enjoy themselves in saying it.

But it's our own faults, thought Rosalind as she tried yet again to settle to her drawing-board. Bernard's and mine. Mine most of all. I ought never to have spoken to him after he gave that lecture.

The day wore on and still she could not decide whether to go to the meeting. If she didn't go it would be said that she was avoiding him and if she did go no doubt one or the other of them would provide fresh fuel for the story. By the time Martin was due to get home from school she had definitely decided not to go to the meeting but to salve her conscience by doing the other thing that she was shirking, which was to challenge Martin about the stolen plants without having faked any evidence. Even if she met with a blank denial from him, she would have done her best.

At six o'clock there was no sign of Martin. At half past six Rosalind began to be seriously worried. At seven o'clock she telephoned Deirdre's home, something she had never done before because she knew Martin didn't like it. The bell rang and rang in an empty house. By this time Rosalind was feeling deeply lonely and depressed as well as anxious. So great was her need for kindly human company that she was about to walk along the lane to the police house and ask Arthur whether there had been any accident in the locality when she remembered that Arthur would not be there: only the relief constable. Arthur would be at Lesley's place. Rosalind was hesitating about going there after all when the telephone rang and she snatched it up.

"That you, Mum?" said Martin's voice.

Rosalind felt faint with relief. "Hullo, darling. Not coming home to eat?"

It took considerable heroism to produce the casual tone of voice. Martin's own voice sounded quite clear, but somehow a little guarded, as if he were not alone.

"I'll probably be quite late," he said. "I'm sorry I couldn't let you know before but I wasn't sure what I was doing. Hope you haven't gone and cooked anything."

"Nothing special," said Rosalind brightly. She was more convinced than ever that there was somebody with Martin and almost equally sure that it was not Deirdre. There was a very faint sound coming over the wire that sounded like a giggle, and Deirdre never giggled. Besides, if Martin were with Deirdre he would say so. With an enormous effort she stopped herself from asking where he was, and said instead: "Everything all right?"

"Fine," he replied.

"Good. See you later then."

"See you later, Mum. Be good."

He rang off.

All of a sudden the cottage which had been Rosalind's haven became intolerable to her and she could not endure to remain for another moment between its four walls. She picked up her handbag, ran out of the front door, and slammed it behind her. After standing in the porch for a minute or two she recovered enough to open the door again, check that she had turned off the gas cooker, and pick up a jacket in case it should have turned cool by the time she came home. To get to Lesley Green's bungalow she would have to walk along the main street of the village, past the village hall and half a mile further, taking about fifteen minutes in all. Committee members had been invited to come at seven for one of Lesley's buffet suppers, but the meeting itself was not likely to start until nearer eight and she would be in time for that.

As she shut the gate behind her Rosalind remembered that she had forgotten to pick up the envelope containing the agenda and other papers, but the thought of returning to the cottage a second time was more than she could endure. Perhaps there would be a spare copy. But in any case she felt in no fit state of mind to talk intelligently about estimates for the extension or the problems of vandalism. To be able to look as if she was listening to the discussion was the most she could hope for. When she came to the gates leading to the car park of the village hall Rosalind paused for a moment and stared at the building, trying to remember what all the discussion was about. Had somebody suggested a squash court? Or was it badminton? At any rate it couldn't be any sport that Martin was keen on or she would have been thinking about it for his sake.

Or would she? Wasn't she a most unnatural and unloving mother to collect evidence against her son? Surely most mothers would refuse to believe that their children could do anything seriously wrong until it had been proved beyond all doubt.

As she stood there, looking at the village hall but not seeing it, Rosalind felt a return of the paralysing doubt and insecurity that had so distressed her after her acquittal, and the prospect of sitting in a room full of people became even more terrifying than that of remaining at home tormented by her suspicions of

Martin. She was released from this paralysis by the sound of a car drawing up to the kerb and it was with a sense that fate was proving too strong for her that she recognized Bernard's white Renault.

"Going to the meeting? Like a lift?" He was determinedly casual.

"Thanks, but don't you think it would be better if we didn't arrive together?" said Rosalind in the same tone of voice.

"Oh. It's started, has it?" He sounded angry now.

"I think so."

"Then get in." Bernard opened the door. "We might as well give them something to gossip about. You look as if you could do with a bit of cheering up. We're not going to that bloody meeting. We're going out to dinner. I've been in London all afternoon and I haven't been home yet and I could do with a meal, not just snippets. So could you."

Rosalind said nothing. By getting into the car she had agreed to everything. When they had been driving for about ten minutes in what seemed to be a northerly direction she said: "We're not going in to Brighton then?"

"No. Too many people. Too rackety. What you want is peace. There's a little country pub somewhere round here. Good but not yet trendy. Only hope I can find it."

He turned off into a side road and then again into an even narrower and very twisting lane. Rosalind lost all sense of direction.

"Are you going to ring Lesley?" she asked as they pulled up in front of a very unassuming-looking square red-brick building. "They'll be terribly disappointed if you don't turn up and send no message."

Bernard did not reply and she had the feeling that her remark had irritated him, but she could not guess why. As they walked into the bar she had a moment of panic. I don't know this man, she said to herself; I know practically nothing about him, and yet I am flinging away all the life I have built up with such pains for Martin and myself.

The bar was airy and not at all noisy and the ten or twelve people drinking and eating there took no notice of Rosalind and Bernard. When they had ordered their drinks and made their selection from the menu Bernard said, "Excuse me a moment" and disappeared. Rosalind felt a fresh wave of panic as she sat alone. The conviction that in some way Bernard was going to bring disaster on her own life and Martin's was overwhelming. He was absent for longer than she had expected and when he returned the fit of irritation seemed to have passed and he was smiling.

"This is going to prove a very expensive evening," he said as they took their places at a table.

"Expensive?" Rosalind looked puzzled and he laughed outright.

"Poor Rosalind. Were you thinking I grudged you a very modestly priced meal? No, my love. I'm not talking about money. I'm thinking of what I've had to promise Miss Lesley Green in order to get her to forgive me for playing truant this evening. Item, open one bazaar. Item, give two more talks. Item, attend an occasional committee meeting. She drives a hard bargain, that delightfully intelligent lady who makes such delicious elderberry wine."

"I didn't realize you'd gone to telephone," said Rosalind in a rather dazed manner.

"You thought I was quite incapable of civilized behaviour?"

Rosalind shook her head.

"And that I needed to be reminded to be courteous? You don't really trust me, do you, Rosalind?"

"I suppose not," she said unhappily.

"Then that makes two of us, because I don't trust you an inch. If Martin were ever in trouble I expect you would fight like a tigress in defence of her young, not caring whom she devoured in the process."

Rosalind simply shook her head again.

"You wouldn't? Why not?"

"Because I'm an unnatural mother, I suppose," she exclaimed in desperation.

"What makes you think that?"

Rosalind did not reply.

"I can quite understand if you don't want to tell me anything about—" began Bernard and broke off as the girl brought their soup.

"Though actually there's no need for you to tell me," he continued when they were alone again, "because I can more or less guess what's been going on. Would you like me to tell you instead?"

"I thought," said Rosalind, finding her voice at last and discovering it was rather shaky, "that the point of this dinner was to have a break from it all." She picked up her spoon and immediately laid it down again, took a white paper napkin from the tumbler and said, "Sorry, it seems that I am about to weep into my soup."

"Go ahead," said Bernard. "Don't mind me." And he began on his with every appearance of enjoying it. After a couple of minutes Rosalind did the same.

"You're very good for me," she said with a smile. "You know, I really *like* you. You have a rare capacity for keeping emotions at a tolerable level."

"That's only because I'm a heartless beast."

"Not true," said Rosalind firmly, and they continued with their meal in silence. Bernard was half-way through his salmon mayonnaise and Rosalind not far behind when she looked up and caught him looking at her with an expression that was almost tender. To smile back was an involuntary reflex action.

"Have you read any good books lately?" he asked.

Rosalind began to laugh. "Only *The Trial and Death of Socrates*," she said.

Bernard put down his knife and fork and clutched at his forehead with both hands in exaggerated despair.

"Here it comes again. That bloody hemlock. Keeps popping up all over the place. Grows and grows till we can't see anything else. Like those horror plants in *The Day of the Triffids*." He picked up his knife and fork and began to eat again. "Well at least there's none of it in this salad."

Rosalind peered a trifle anxiously at her plate before taking the next mouthful. Then she said with an air of decision: "I don't think Martin is planning to use it as a garnish. It's the juice he is interested in."

"Juice," said Bernard in a noncommittal voice.

"Yes. Hemlock and/or hemlock water dropwort juice. What are we going to do about it, Bernard?"

—— 15 ——

"I'm quite sure," said Bernard twenty minutes later when they were drinking their coffee, "that neither Jane nor Garry nor Martin has any intention of trying to poison me. Look," he continued as Rosalind still seemed unconvinced, "let's take opportunity and motive in the good old-fashioned way. Both Jane and Garry have had plenty of opportunities. Why have they never tried to do it? Because neither wants me dead. They both hate me in their respective ways but they don't want me out of the way. They want to see me having great troubles, as I told you before."

"But Martin has a motive," said Rosalind. "He's bitterly jealous of you. He really does wish you out of the way."

"Possibly, but not in the way that leads to action. It's like a child crying 'I wish you were dead.' It doesn't mean much. A sort of dramatic adolescent gesture. In any case, where is his opportunity?"

Rosalind didn't answer for a moment and she could feel Bernard's eyes on her as she stared down at the dark oak table top. Telling Bernard about Martin had eased her mind, but only at the cost of greatly increasing her feeling of guilt towards her son. That Bernard should be trying so hard to reassure her and showing understanding for Martin was no comfort. Martin wouldn't want Bernard to understand him and make allowances for him. He'd much prefer Bernard to feel the straight anger and jealousy that he felt himself, a man to man thing, and not a man to child.

"Martin isn't a child," she said aloud.

"You haven't answered my question," retorted Bernard. "How do you expect him to find the opportunity to poison me?"

"I've got a suspicion that he's at Bell House this evening," said Rosalind, and proceeded to tell him about Martin's telephone call.

"In that case he's probably being seduced by Jane. She's still very good at it, in spite of alcoholism and neurotic fears. Curious, isn't it, that the sex drive seems to be totally unaffected although the whole personality is so twisted and damaged."

Rosalind looked him straight in the eye. "I know you only talk in this way to cover up your own disgust," she said, "but I wish you wouldn't do it. I find it quite horrible."

"I'm sorry. It's habit, I suppose. One lives so long with this sort of spiky armour around oneself that it's difficult to shed it. You could help me shed it, though, Rosalind. You know that, don't you?"

"Perhaps I could, but what's the use of talking about it? You've got a wife and you say you've no intention of leaving her. Strange as it may seem, I've got certain objections to having an affair with a married man. Not to mention the total impossibility of keeping any secret in Swallowfields. It's hopeless, Bernard. We've made a frightful hash of it."

"It needn't have been hopeless. Jane liked you when she met you at that meeting. She'd have accepted you as a colleague working with me on my books. Oh, of course there'd have been jealousies and scenes, but you're tactful enough to have made it work. We could have done a lot for each other, you and I, even in such circumstances."

"So you think," said Rosalind, speaking with controlled anger, "that that is a worthy situation to offer a woman whom you profess to care for and who desperately needs a secure social position."

"I think we'd better go back to the car to discuss this further," said Bernard.

He paid the bill and they left the building without speaking to each other. When they had driven a little way back along the winding lane he turned into the entrance to a field and stopped the car.

"Would you marry me if I were free?" he asked.

"I don't know," said Rosalind. "I suppose it depends."

"On whether you could feel quite sure that I had not killed off Jane in order to be free, I suppose," he said.

Rosalind turned in her seat to look at him closely. An interesting, intelligent face, its lines harsh now, but quickly softening when he put on his charming public self. A difficult, edgy, bitter man, not to many people's taste if they really got to know him, but surely not a potential murderer.

Not yet, at any rate. Would she be turning him into one if she told the truth now, that of course she would want to marry him, whatever the circumstances?

"I believe I could come to love you very much," she said at last, "and I believe that we could be happy and could greatly help each other, but I don't see how we can ignore the circumstances that we are trapped in. Don't you think the best thing now is for me to go away for a few weeks? I've got an old uncle and aunt I go and stay with occasionally. I could take Martin if he wanted to come and if not, I'd leave him here on his own. Meanwhile you could try to sort yourself out and decide whether you feel able to part from Jane in some legal manner."

"I don't see why you should have to go away. You won't be able to work and you'll lose some of your income. You can't afford that."

"All right then. Clear out yourself. Surely you can get fixed up to give some lectures somewhere."

Bernard made no reply.

"I see," said Rosalind quietly. "You're frightened of leaving Jane. You think she could drink herself to death while you're gone and it'll be on your conscience for ever afterwards."

"I suppose so," said Bernard miserably. Then he added in a voice harsh with anger and frustration: "What incredible creatures we humans are! I really believe that I could more easily kill Jane quickly and painlessly than I could leave her alone to do the same thing more slowly and painfully herself."

"A clinic?" suggested Rosalind, with the sensation that the tunnel was closing in on her again. "Or a nursing home of some sort?"

"If there were any hope of getting Jane to agree to go to such a place, don't you think I'd have done something about it ages ago?"

"Yes, of course. I'm sorry. If that's the way it is, then I don't see much point in my rushing off to my aunt's either, since obviously you won't be able to use the time I'm away to any good effect. I'll look around for a house as far as possible from Swallowfields and move as soon as I can and go right out of your life. Meanwhile we'd better keep apart."

Bernard said nothing and Rosalind turned her head again to see that he had rested both arms on the steering-wheel and had buried his face in them. He made no sound nor movement but she knew at once that he was weeping. She looked away again and stared across the field of young green corn, shining bright in the evening sun. Then she shut her eyes for a moment as if taking farewell of the beauties of the world, twisted round in the passenger seat and put her arms around him, shifting him until his head rested against her shoulder, and murmuring comforting words as if to a child.

"It's all right," she said. "I'm not going away. I'm going to stay here whatever happens. I'll be here when you need me. Always. Whatever you say, whatever you do. It doesn't matter. I'll never leave you. Whenever you want to come and see me, I'll be there."

They remained like this until the red sphere of the sun had almost reached the horizon and then Bernard suddenly pulled himself upright, started the car with a jerk, and drove back to Swallowfields at a dangerous speed without speaking a word. It was twilight when they pulled up at the cottage by the church.

"There's no light," said Rosalind. "Martin can't be back yet. I'm afraid you're going to find him at Bell House."

"If I do find him with Jane I promise to behave myself," said Bernard stiffly.

"Of course you will. Good night and thank you." She kissed

him lightly and opened the door. "Don't forget. I'm always here."

"I won't forget," he said without looking at her.

Rosalind came into the cottage with the feeling of having been absent for months and not hours. When Martin came in a little later she was still sitting in the dark of the living-room, staring at the uncurtained window. He seemed to be in a state of near euphoria, flushed and restless.

"You do look a poor old thing," he said as she shrank in the sudden glare of the central light that he had switched on. "What you need is a drink. Have we got any booze in this dump?"

It was Martin talking and yet it was not like Martin. Jane's influence was obvious and equally obviously he had already had plenty to drink.

"What I want is bed," said Rosalind firmly. "I wasn't feeling very well and I fell asleep in the chair, which is always a mistake. One wakes feeling worse than ever."

"Why didn't you tell me you weren't well when I phoned?" said Martin. "I'd have come home earlier."

"I didn't want to spoil your fun," said Rosalind. "Good night, darling. Sleep well."

From her own bedroom, through two closed doors, she could hear him singing loudly. Then he switched on the radio equally loudly and it was a long time before the house was quiet enough for her to try to sleep.

— 16 —

Nearly a week later, after seeing nothing of Bernard and having still said nothing to Martin about the plants, Rosalind received a letter from Jane.

> Do bring yourself and Martin to dinner on Saturday, [it ran,] and let me entertain you properly, since that last occasion wasn't quite all that might be desired. It would be a real kindness to me because Bernard is pining to see you and is more bad-tempered than ever, and Garry has gone all mysterious and peculiar these last few days. Can you imagine what it's like for a woman with my going out phobia to be shut up with two such unsatisfactory creatures? To see a symphathetic human being like yourself would be a great treat, so please say yes, and bring your nice handsome son as well.

Rosalind wasted very little time in trying to decide whether this invitation was on Jane's initiative or whether it had been instigated by Bernard. She was relieved to receive it, because it rescued her from the state of limbo in which she had been since her parting with Bernard. Heroic gestures need a quick follow-up, sacrifices offered need instant acceptance if the offerer is not to experience an intolerable feeling of anti-climax. Such a feeling had been oppressing Rosalind for days.

141

She had made her decision and finally committed herself while she held Bernard weeping in her arms, and had felt a great surge of courage and strength. But so far there had been no call upon it. It was as if she had taken a great leap into a raging sea, only to find herself caught up on a ledge with no possibility of returning to safe ground and no means of plunging further down the cliff. She went about her normal activities in a preoccupied and listless manner, grateful that Martin was so little at home, and trying to avoid contact with her acquaintances in the village.

Every now and then she would find herself catching glimpses of what life could be like for Bernard and herself, but when these glimpses began to turn into more specific daydreaming she stamped on it firmly and began to paint or read or do some domestic job, only to find that the glimpses returned with greater urgency than before.

When she dialled the number of Bell House it was as if a safety-valve had been opened. The phone rang for some time before Jane's voice answered. She sounded slightly breathless.

"Sorry to be so long," she said. "I was out in the summer-house. Garry was actually in here cleaning the hall but of course he's no use to us for answering the phone."

Rosalind could not help wondering whether Garry was actually standing by at this moment, but she thought it wiser not to mention him.

"We'd love to come to dinner," she said, "but please don't go to any great trouble for us."

Honeyed falseness, she said to herself as she was speaking. It was the sort of thing she normally loathed and avoided. But in her present mood she had no objection to talking in this way. She even took some satisfaction in it. It was as if she were sacrificing her own integrity and honesty for Bernard's sake, and that was all that mattered.

"My dear," said Jane in similar gushing tones, "it won't be my trouble I assure you. Garry does all the cooking now. He's become quite an expert and he'd be bitterly offended if I told him to do something simple. I give him carte blanche so you'll just have to take your chance. I think I can promise that he

won't actually poison you," she concluded with her character-
istic little giggle.

Rosalind laughed too. She was indeed feeling quite light-
hearted at the prospect of this dinner-party, which must surely
at the very least be intensely embarrassing and at the worst be
disastrous in some as yet unknown manner.

"I've asked Miss Green to come in for coffee afterwards,"
went on Jane. "She seems to be a leading light in this locality,
and it's time we asked her, but I didn't feel I could face any
more to dinner. It'll be quite a triumph for me to sit at table
with the four of us, you know."

She paused for Rosalind's sympathetic murmur.

"Of course you understand. I knew from the very moment I
saw you that you were the sort of person to understand about
that sort of thing. In fact I couldn't even face this dinner-party
if it were anyone else but you and Martin. He's such a dear
boy. You know he's been sitting with me several evenings
when Bernard's been in town till late. Didn't he tell you? Isn't
that just like him! Keeping his good deeds a secret even from
his own mother. He's so modest. That's what I like about him.
And so patient with a stupid old woman like me when he
explains all about his studies. Of course I don't understand
anything about physics or chemistry but I do think one ought to
try to listen when a youngster is so enthusiastic, don't you? Oh
dear. I was forgetting. Of course you must be very busy with
your painting and wouldn't have so much free time as I have to
pay attention to him."

Rosalind was unprepared for this particular form of attack
and had some difficulty in replying. Her awkwardness seemed
to satisfy Jane, however, because the latter continued in an
even more complacent tone of voice: "I do think an older
woman can do so much for a boy of Martin's age, don't you?
They are so uncertain of themselves at that stage, particularly
if they have no father. They badly need someone who will help
convince them that they really are grown-up men and not
children any longer."

Jane continued along these lines for some time, rather to
Rosalind's relief because it saved her from the effort of finding
further replies. Eventually, no doubt judging that she had

stuck enough pins into her victim, she changed key and reverted to her pathetic and helpless self.

"Do tell me, Rosalind," she said, "whether I have done the right thing in inviting the village policeman to come in for coffee too. I knew I had to ask Miss Green, but a police constable! It does seem rather odd, but Bernie says he's on the village hall committee so I suppose he must be socially acceptable. I mean, I hope I'm not a snob, but after all, one wouldn't ask the milkman. I mean, it would embarrass him, wouldn't it?"

"Has Arthur accepted?" asked Rosalind.

"Arthur!" Jane gave a little squeal of delight. "Isn't that sweet? He would be called Arthur, wouldn't he? So solid and comfortable. I'm sure we shall all feel much safer when he's in the house. What a pity I can't ask him to dinner, but I think even Bernie would think that is going too far. He never used to be so democratic, you know. It's only since we came to live in the country the he's decided we ought to mix with absolutely everybody. Of course village society is rather limited and one has very little choice."

Rosalind decided that she would give herself the pleasure of naming a few well-known people who lived in the locality, but Jane's answer to that was to start talking about her own fears of social contact.

"I think it's very brave of you to give this dinner-party," said Rosalind, reverting to her sweet manner, "and to invite two extra guests in afterwards. And since one of them is Chairman of the Village Hall Committee, it is perfectly in order to invite the Secretary too, even if he does happen to be the village policeman. Incidentally, I know him quite well. He's a delightful person and a great gardener. I don't think you will find conversation will be difficult."

"Oh, I'm not worried about that," said Jane. "I'm sure we shall be able to provide him with something of interest— perhaps even of professional interest."

Rosalind pondered over this remark when the conversation came to an end at last. There was, as she had said, no reason why Arthur should not take part in a social occasion but she could not help feeling that Jane had some ulterior motive for desiring his presence on this one. Could there be some plot to fake some case against Bernard and accuse him in the presence of a police officer? And if so, was it Jane's own scheme, or thought up by Garry and herself? Or even, horrible thought, by Jane and Martin together? Rosalind longed to talk it over with Bernard. If there were any such plot afoot she could not believe that he had not guessed. Perhaps he had even connived at it in order to force things to a crisis. It could even be that he knew Martin's part in it and was deliberately keeping away from Rosalind in order not to distress her. For there was no doubt that in spite of her firm commitment to Bernard, she was deeply upset by the way that Martin was behaving, both on her own account and on Deirdre's. Jane might be exaggerating about the amount of time that Martin was spending with her, but there was certainly some truth in it. Martin had not brought Deirdre to Swallowfields and had not even mentioned her to his mother since the evening when they went for a moonlight drive together. Had that been to break off their friendship? Rosalind dared not ask him, nor did she feel able to get in touch with Deirdre at her home.

When Martin came home late that evening, she refrained as usual from asking him what he had been doing and said instead: "We've been invited to dinner at Bell House on Saturday and I've accepted for you. I hope that's all right."

"Of course it's all right. I'd like to see Jane again."

It was clumsily said. Martin had no natural gift for dissembling and intrigue, and Rosalind suspected that he had seen Jane very recently and knew all about the invitation already.

"Is anyone else going?" he asked with such elaborate casualness that his mother's suspicions were confirmed.

"Not to dinner, but Lesley and Arthur are coming along afterwards," she replied.

"Sounds exciting. Are we going to play Murder? Or produce a body in the library to be found by the arm of the law?"

Rosalind got up from her chair in the living-room and switched off the reading-lamp. "I don't think that's particularly funny," she said coldly, "and neither do you really. Do you?"

"No doubt my humour is too adolescent for you," said

Martin. "I'm sorry I can't match up to your degree of sophistication."

Rosalind glanced at his sulky angry face and felt a curious little pang of something that was as much joy as pain. It was many days since they had been as close as they were at this moment. Had they come together in affection and good fellowship it would of course have been much happier, but to meet in anger was far better than not to meet at all. At least there was feeling between them again; at least they were keenly aware of each other and not moving around the cottage like zombies.

Martin had flopped down into an armchair. Rosalind came across and put an arm round his shoulders and with her other hand stroked his hair.

"Tell me, darling," she murmured. "Please tell me. Tell Teddy and me together."

This was a magic phrase from Martin's childhood. It had never failed to elicit from the little boy what it was that was troubling him. For a few moments, while Martin remained silent but did not push her away, Rosalind believed that its magic was going to work now. If he tells me, she said to herself, and if I have to let Bernard down in order to help Martin, I'm sure Bernard will understand. I really meant what I said in the car . . . if it came to the crunch I'll stand by him . . . but meanwhile if Martin needs me . . .

Martin raised his head at last, grinned at her with a flash of his old self, and said brightly: "There's nothing to tell, Mum. I'm fine. Aren't you?"

"I'm all right," she said, both disappointed and relieved at the same time. "Why shouldn't I be?"

"No reason at all. You aren't waiting on tenterhooks for your exam results."

"No, thank God. Well, I hope you're managing to amuse yourself and take your mind off them." It was the nearest she dared go to asking him where he was spending his spare time.

"I'm amusing myself all right." He gave a great yawn. "I'm going to bed."

The chance had passed by. They were back where they had been all the week—strangers living in the same house, but

Rosalind felt that this time, at any rate, she really had done her best to break through to him.

At about eleven o'clock the next morning the telephone rang and Bernard's voice asked, "Are you alone?"

"Yes," said Rosalind. "Where are you?"

"In the library at the shed. I can see Jane and Garry through the little window. At the moment they are inspecting the little herb garden near the summer-house but if either of them shows signs of going within reach of a phone extension I'll ring off at once and try again later. Two things, Rosalind. First, I want to thank you for what you did and said the other night. It meant more to me than even you will ever be able to understand. Second, I've been trying to take your advice to get away for a while and have been spending much of last week with some old friends of mine in London. A former colleague and her husband. Peaceful and sensible people. We've talked things over a lot. That's your doing, dear Rosalind. Thawing me out sufficiently to be able to ask advice from good friends instead of being too frozen with pride to ask for help. So I must thank you for that too."

"And what was their advice?" asked Rosalind.

"They've too much sense to try to advise," said Bernard, "knowing what a hopelessly contrary person I am, but they did help to clear my mind and convince me that this marriage of mine has got to come to an end for both Jane's sake and my own and that I have got to try to stop making other people unhappy. You can shut yourself up in an intolerable situation if you feel so guilty that you have to punish yourself in that way, but you shouldn't expect other people to share your prison. That's the message and a very good one too."

"But, Bernard," began Rosalind, frightened of where this conversation was leading, "you remember what I said. That I'd accept it and do my best to cope with it as it was."

"Yes, my love. I'll never forget what you said. It's like music in my mind. But I'm being purely selfish now. I've not so many years of life left and I don't want to waste them in this way. Not now that I've met you. I've got to break out of the prison and I'm going to do it. But I have to do it without your help. Please understand me, Rosalind."

"I understand you," said Rosalind, biting back the question: what are you going to do?

"Thank you," he said. "Hang on a moment—can't see from here." A few seconds later he added: "Garry's gone round the side of the house. I'll have to ring off. I gather we're meeting for dinner tommorrow. I don't know what Jane is planning but no doubt you'll come prepared for anything. How are things with Martin?"

"Pretty awful."

"I'm sorry. Goodbye for now."

The line went dead, leaving Rosalind feeling sick with frustration and apprehension and curiosity and a host of other sensations. The hours to be got through until the following evening seemed to be more heavily weighted than any hours she could remember in her life, and in her mind she lived through an infinite variety of dinner-parties at Bell House and their aftermaths. But of course the thing that actually happens is always the very thing you haven't thought of, she told herself when the moment arrived at last.

— 17 —

Jane had certainly told the truth about Garry's cooking. He had concentrated on one hot dish, a navarin of lamb, followed by a lemon mousse, cheese and dessert.

"It's absolutely delicious," said Rosalind after taking a few mouthfuls with a certain amount of trepidation. "I believe I can taste the rosemary—that's traditional for the dish, isn't it?—but I can't begin to guess at the other herbs."

"Have a try," said Bernard, beaming at her.

He was being a perfect host. Even Martin's surly greeting to him and the fact that Jane had obviously had plenty to drink could not entirely take away from the pleasantly festive atmosphere as they sat down at the oval table in the dining-room, Bernard facing the window that looked out on the back garden, Jane at the other end of the table with her face in shadow, with Martin on her right and Rosalind on her left.

Garry waited on them efficiently and unobtrusively, but Rosalind was shocked to see how pale and ill the boy looked. There was no sign of the broad mysterious smile that had so struck her when she first saw him and before she knew that he could not speak. His brown eyes seemed darker than ever, sunken and full of some intense and inexpressible emotion.

When he took away her plate for the main course Rosalind turned and smiled up at him and said: "Thank you, Garry. I enjoyed that very much indeed."

She hoped she didn't sound patronizing, and she had the

impression that there was a flicker of response from those speechless lips. But it might have been due to anger or frustration. It was impossible to tell. Bernard followed her lead and praised the meal, but Jane and Martin said nothing to Garry, and Rosalind thought she caught a significant look pass between them.

"More wine?" said Bernard, picking up the bottle of rosé and holding it poised over her glass.

"No, thank you."

Rosalind drank only one glass and Bernard only water. Martin and Jane finished the rest of the bottle. Neither of them took much part in the conversation for the first part of the meal. Jane produced one or two little digs at Rosalind that were not difficult to ignore, and Martin answered if a question was directly addressed to him but otherwise said nothing. Bernard and Rosalind kept up a mild conversation about village affairs, gardening, and the news of the day. It could have passed for a tolerably successful social occasion. Not until they were all four sitting in the big room at the front of the house did Jane begin her attack.

"The others won't be here just yet," said Bernard. "Shall we wait for them? Or have some coffee straight away?"

"Better wait," said Jane. "Garry's in a filthy temper. He'll probably refuse to make coffee."

"He made a delicious dinner," said Rosalind since nobody else seemed inclined to speak.

"So you said before," retorted Jane. Her voice was clear, but Rosalind had the impression that she was not fully in control of what she was saying, whether because she had been drinking steadily before dinner, or whether because of some repressed excitement, or simply because of nervous tension. Martin had seated himself near to her in a protective manner. He was flushed and looked as if it would not take much to irritate him into hasty and ill-considered speech.

"Isn't there a quotation or something," went on Jane addressing herself to Martin, "about it being rather suspicious if somebody keeps going on about something? That it really means they're thinking the opposite, I mean. I'm sure you'll know it. I'm much too stupid to remember."

" 'The lady doth protest too much, methinks.' It comes from *Hamlet*. The play scene. Hamlet's mother says it after hearing the queen in the play swear that if her husband dies she will never never marry again." Martin began to laugh rather wildly. "Very appropriate, Jane. We all know what Hamlet's mother did after Claudius had killed Hamlet's father."

Jane gave a little hiccup. "Pardon me, folks," she said, and then added: "Married the murderer, didn't she? Hamlet's mother, I mean. What do you know, Martin? Perhaps I'm cleverer than I think. Don't you think I'm clever, Bernie?"

"I think we'll have some coffee now, after all," said Bernard. He got up. "I'll go and help Garry."

Rosalind stood up too. The thought of being left alone in the room with Martin and Jane was intolerable. "Can I do anything?" she asked.

"No thanks," said Bernard. "I won't be a moment."

"Bring me something to drink!" cried Jane as he left the room.

"Get it yourself," he replied without turning round.

"What would you like, Jane?" asked Martin. "Shall I get it for you?"

Jane did not immediately reply. She was staring after Bernard, her hands gripping the arms of the chair. The expression on her face deprived it of all its former beauty.

She's as likely to murder him as he her, thought Rosalind. He's got to part from her and bring this to an end. But the thought of how it might be brought to an end made her feel sick with fear.

"No thanks, darling," she heard Jane say to Martin. "I'll wait till the others come and have my drink then. You'll all have to have that poisonous elderberry stuff. I'll be sticking to apricot brandy. A new bottle. Untouched." She laughed. "You can join me if you're scared of the other rubbish, Martin. Let them poison themselves."

" 'Poison in jest,' " said Martin.

"Come again?"

"It's from the same scene in *Hamlet*. He's referring to the play. He tells Claudius that there's no offence in it. It's all in jest. Poison in jest."

"Gosh," said Jane looking very impressed. "You really do know your Shakespeare, don't you? I call that pretty good for a scientist."

"Not really," said Martin. "It's only *Hamlet* that I know. I've been re-reading it because it seemed relevant. I mean, I think I can understand how Hamlet feels."

Martin glanced at his mother as he said these last words. It was by no means a friendly glance and Jane made it even worse by giving an audible gasp and saying, "Oh Martin!" in pretended reproach.

Rosalind, who had very much expected this sort of thing, still found herself almost uncontrollably pained by it. Bernard's return saved her from having to decide whether to hit back or not.

"Garry's bringing the coffee," he said. "Does anybody want some music while we wait for the others?"

Jane and Martin looked at each other and began to laugh. Bernard raised his eyebrows but made no comment.

"Rosalind?" he asked, turning to her.

After a moment's thought Rosalind decided that it would probably make matters worse to put on a record. "It's hardly worth it, is it," she said, "just for a minute or two. Lesley and Arthur can't be long now."

Jane and Martin laughed again. "Enter the law," said Jane.

"The long arm of the law," added Martin. "Here it comes. Wait for it!" He stood up and held up a hand as if halting traffic.

In the silence that followed, the sound of tyres on the gravel was clearly heard. It was followed by a ring of the front doorbell and a moment later Arthur's voice could be heard in the hall.

"Hullo, Garry. I hear you carried off all of the honours at darts. We'll have to get you into the team."

In the midst of all her preoccupations Rosalind was conscious of surprise. Garry and darts? It had never occurred to her that the boy had any life outside Bell House at all. She wondered if any of the others were equally surprised, but Martin and Jane were looking at each other again, sharing their secret excitement, and Bernard had moved across the room to greet Arthur. The mask of host had momentarily slipped from his face and Rosalind caught an expression of misery and despair that made her heart contract.

Arthur looked as comfortable and at home as he did in any surroundings but Rosalind felt sure that his keen eye had missed none of the tension in the room.

"Miss Green is going to be a little late," he said after greeting everybody. "She sends her apologies."

"Then we won't wait any longer," said Bernard. "Come on, Garry. Put the tray down here."

The tray was a large one and almost completely covered the low table. On it was a coffee-pot and milk jug, six cups and saucers, six glasses, biscuits and chocolate peppermints, and two bottles, a large one almost half full of a dark purple liquid and a smaller one with a screw top whose contents were a golden yellow.

Jane watched impatiently as Garry arranged the contents of the tray, moving some of them to other low tables.

"Is that the apricot brandy you got for me?" she asked Garry. "Are you sure you've put out a new bottle?"

All eyes in the room went to the bottle that Garry was placing on the table near to Jane's chair. It was quite full of the golden liquid. Jane stretched out a hand to it and then as if suddenly remembering her guests, withdrew her hand again and sat on the edge of the chair, watching Garry's movements impatiently. Nobody else spoke. They were all watching the mute boy as if hypnotized by him, or as if determined not to notice the condition Jane was in.

At last he had arranged everything to his satisfaction and with one final glance around he turned and left the room. There was an audible easing of tension after he had gone. Bernard began to pour out the coffee and hand it round and Jane grabbed the smaller bottle and unscrewed the top. Her hand trembled as she started to pour out, and Martin got up and did it for her. Jane picked up her glass and raised it to her lips.

"I thought we'd better produce Lesley's wine," Bernard was

saying, "and actually it's very good, but if anybody would rather have a liqueur with their coffee . . ."

"Yes, I think I would rather," said Rosalind.

"If that's apricot brandy, suits me," said Arthur.

"And me," said Martin.

"All right, then. We'll do our duty by Lesley later on," said Bernard. "Thanks, Martin. I'll leave you to dispense since you've started the job."

Martin seemed to be glad of the little task. Rosalind noticed him glance at Jane, but it seemed to be as much in disappointment as in disgust. For Jane's moment of going right over the edge seemed to have coincided with the drinking of the glass of apricot brandy. As Rosalind remembered so well from her own experience, it was not uncommon for somebody with an alcohol problem like Jane's to continue drinking steadily for a considerable time without showing any great effect, and then for the collapse to come suddenly, the last little drink being the last straw. Jane's collapse appeared imminent. She was slumped back in the chair, her eyes open but unfocused and unseeing, and the empty liqueur glass was lying in her lap, no longer gripped by the limp fingers.

Rosalind saw Bernard look at her and saw his face harden. Then he raised his own glass of the liqueur, deliberately ignoring Jane. Taking their cue from him, the others did the same.

"Cheers," he said.

The voices of the other three were drowned by the sound that suddenly came from the doorway. There was nothing human in it. It was loud and bloodcurdling, the cry of some unearthly monster in a horror film. Garry's face looked inhuman too with its fixed grin and staring eyes. His arms were stretched out in the agony of his own crying. Bernard and Arthur, Rosalind and Martin, all looked at him appalled, their drinks untouched. The noise came again, not quite so loud this time. Garry dropped on to his knees and began to crawl across the carpet towards Jane's chair.

Bernard had gone very white. "I don't think that this is the right moment to drink a friendly toast," he said. "Would you please all put down your glasses and go out into the garden for a few minutes while I attend to my wife? This stage of the proceedings is never very agreeable and with Garry having hysterics it's going to be worse than ever. As soon as I've got her to bed and calmed him down I'll rejoin the party. Please make my apologies to Lesley Green if she comes meanwhile."

All of them put down their liqueur glasses, but only Rosalind made the slightest move to carry out the rest of Bernard's request. She took a step or two in the direction of the door and then, seeing that nobody was going to follow her, paused and turned back. Martin was leaning over Jane's chair, calling her name in a frightened voice and looking very helpless and very young. Garry was grovelling at her feet, caressing her legs. Bernard and Arthur were looking first at Jane and then at each other.

"I'm sorry, Mr. Goodwin," Arthur was saying, "but I've seen plenty of alcoholic collapses too and I'm afraid this one does not look as if the remedy is going to be to sleep it off. So, with your permission, I'll just take a look at your wife."

"Go ahead," said Bernard, barely opening his mouth.

Arthur bent over Jane. Martin, looking more frightened than ever, straightened up and moved away, closer to his mother. Garry got up and ran out of the room, shaking off Bernard's attempts to restrain him.

"Ought we to let him go?" said Rosalind. "If it turns out that . . ." She did not finish.

Bernard shrugged. "I can't stop him. Martin could perhaps. But do you really want the two boys fighting on top of everything else?"

Rosalind made no reply.

Arthur stood up at last and said briefly: "She's dead. Who's your doctor?"

"No one," snapped Bernard. "I'm never ill and Jane refuses to see a doctor."

"So she's not been examined recently?"

"Not within the necessary period, certainly. I believe she last saw a doctor two years ago in London when she had a bad attack of flu."

"That means an inquest, then, I'm afraid," said Arthur.

"I quite realize that," said Bernard stiffly. "You'll want to call your superior, no doubt. And the police surgeon."

"That would be best," admitted Arthur.

"Go ahead then." Bernard gestured to the telephone extension on the table by the side of the fireplace. "It's all yours. We're at your service and I assure you I won't run away."

18

Rosalind's first reaction was one of sheer physical relief that something had happened at last and that the period of waiting and apprehension was over. Her second reaction, following on so close to the first that it merged with it and became indistinguishable from it, was an immense gratitude that it was Jane and not Bernard who was the victim. Only after she had experienced this great flow of relief did she begin to feel the guilt and the fear. The fear was equally divided between Bernard and Martin. She feared intensely for them both and there was no longer any question of trying to choose between them.

"Where's the dumb lad?" asked Arthur when he had finished telephoning.

"He's probably gone to earth in the garden or in the annexe," said Bernard. "I don't think he'll have gone far."

"I hope not," said Arthur. "I'm sure all this is going to be quickly cleared up, but if there should be any doubts raised, it'll be much better if nobody runs away."

His voice was as mild and reassuring as it always was, but there was an unmistakable threat behind it.

"Oh God, I can't bear it!" cried Martin suddenly. He sat down in a chair some distance from Jane and held his head in his hands.

"Darling!" Rosalind went to him and put an arm round his shoulders.

"Is there something you would like to tell me?" asked Arthur.

Martin gave a loud sob.

"If you can throw any light on Mrs. Goodwin's death it will be best for you to say so at once," persisted Arthur kindly but firmly. "Inspector Peters will be here shortly. He's a young fellow and he'll be grateful to have all the help you can give him."

"Why is she dead?" asked Martin, raising his head for a moment.

"That's what we've got to find out," said Arthur.

Martin jumped to his feet and looked around wildly. "She was poisoned," he shouted, "and I know who did it."

Arthur took him firmly by the arm. "Come now. That's not helping at all, going on like that. You'll only upset your mother and you wouldn't want to do that, would you?"

Martin subsided into the chair again and began to cry audibly. Arthur gave Rosalind an enquiring look.

"I think perhaps he may be able to be of some help," she said in a strangled voice. "And perhaps I can help too. Shall we wait till the Inspector comes?"

"That would be best. It's his enquiry and let's hope it will soon be over. But I'll always be around, of course, if anyone wants to come and talk to me. There they are."

Arthur left the room. For a short while Bernard and Martin and Rosalind were alone.

"You poisoned her!" cried Martin, looking up and glaring at Bernard.

Bernard shook his head. "We've eaten and drunk the same things and only Jane was affected. The only thing she's had that we haven't is the apricot brandy. And we were just about to drink it when Garry came in."

"And stopped us," said Martin. "Very convenient. Saved you thinking up a reason why we shouldn't drink. Or perhaps you put him up to it."

Rosalind rounded on Martin. "If you will just try to use your reason for a moment," she cried, waving aside Bernard's attempts to stop her, "you will see just how idiotic your remarks are. Nobody could possibly have known in advance who was going to drink the apricot brandy and when. Anyway we don't even know yet that there's anything wrong with it. Jane may have had a heart attack."

"She didn't have a heart attack!" shouted Martin. "She was poisoned!"

"Poisoned, eh?" said a new voice. It belonged to the man who came into the room with Arthur. He was dark and thin-faced and looked rather like a ferret. The village constable looked very big beside him.

"Detective-Inspector Peters," said the newcomer. "Mr. Goodwin?"

His voice was quite unsuited to his modest stature. It had the ring of a sergeant-major about it. Bernard only just managed to stop himself from stepping forward and saluting.

"I'm Bernard Goodwin," he said, "and this is Mrs. Bannister and Mr. Martin Bannister."

"Ah," said Detective-Inspector Peters, "the young man who is so convinced that we have a case of malicious poisoning here. Well, I think it would be a good idea if we left all such theories aside for the time being and stick to the facts."

Rosalind found herself taking an instant dislike to Inspector Peters. She had no doubt that Martin felt the same, but on the other hand the ferrety man's words did silence him, and for this Martin's mother was grateful. Stick to the facts they did. Lesley Green, arriving a few minutes later and very anxious to have her say when she had been told the news, was shut up as abruptly as Martin had been. When the Inspector had sufficiently subdued them all and had asked his questions he barked at Arthur.

"Any other witnesses?"

"The mute boy, sir. He came back into the room just before we discovered that the lady was dead."

"Where is he?"

Arthur turned to Bernard.

"Either up in his room or wandering round the garden probably," said the latter.

"Where's his room?"

"Upstairs," said Bernard equally abruptly.

"Perhaps you will show me."

As soon as the Inspector and Bernard had left the room Lesley Green burst out, "What a very rude man!"

"He knows his job," said Arthur.

"He may know his job but there's no need to be so offensive. I thought the police were so concerned about their public image nowadays. After all, we're not criminals."

"Let's be fair, Lesley," said Rosalind. "For all he knows, one of us may be." She turned round suddenly and cried in quite a different sort of voice. "Martin! Where are you going?"

But Martin had already run out of the room.

Rosalind made a gesture of despair. "I'm sorry," she said to Arthur. "I ought not to have let him go."

"You couldn't help it. Don't worry. If you ladies will stay in here I'll go and see what he's up to, and I'll explain to my boss when he comes down." Arthur glanced around the room. "You won't touch anything, will you?"

Both women assured him that they would not, but he continued to look around for a moment or two, as if imprinting the scene on his mind.

After he had gone Lesley walked over to Jane's chair. "She looks just as if she's asleep," she said. "She can't have suffered anything or known she was going to die."

" 'To cease upon the midnight with no pain,' " murmured Rosalind.

"I beg your pardon?"

"Keats's *Ode to a Nightingale*. We had to learn the whole of it at school and it's stuck in my mind ever since. Even at that age I thought it rather self-indulgent. A sort of luxuriating in thoughts of death. Easeful death. That's what he calls it."

"This looks like an easeful death all right," said Lesley. "I hope mine will be no worse. If anyone did poison her, they made quite sure it would be quick and not unpleasant."

Rosalind could not reply. Bernard's words were ringing through her mind. "What curious creatures we humans are . . . I believe I could more easily kill Jane quickly and painlessly than leave her to do it herself slowly and more painfully . . ."

"Well, there's one comfort," Lesley was saying, "I see by the glasses that nobody's yet had any of my elderberry, so the poison can't have been in that. I don't think I'd ever have had the heart to make any again if someone had gone and dropped a lethal dose of hemlock in it."

"Hemlock!" cried Rosalind. "Nobody said anything about hemlock."

"Must be association of ideas," retorted Lesley. "I had to learn the Keats *Ode* too." Then she softened a little. "Look here, Ros, if you know or suspect something, don't you think you ought to tell the police?"

"I've every intention of telling the police anything I know, but they've hardly given me a chance to do so yet."

"No doubt the time will come." Lesley leaned over Jane again. "I say, don't you think it's rather careless of them to leave a couple of possible suspects alone on the scene of the crime, even if Arthur did take such a good look around? We could still fake some evidence if we wanted to."

Rosalind made no reply.

"The fatal glass, for instance. The fatal bottle."

"They've taken the apricot brandy bottle and Jane's glass," pointed out Rosalind.

"But not the others." Lesley bent over one of the untouched liqueur glasses and sniffed at the golden liquid. "I think maybe it has got rather a funny smell. I'm awfully tempted to taste it. D'you think a little sip could really do me any harm, Ros?"

Rosalind was saved from having to reply by the entry of all the rest of the party. Bernard came in first, looking ghastly. He was followed first by the police doctor and the other constable, and then by Martin and Arthur. Martin was gulping and gagging as if he were about to vomit, and the big village constable had him by the arm. The Inspector, looking darker and angrier than ever, came last.

"He'll be all right," said Arthur to Rosalind. "It was just the shock of finding Garry."

"Finding Garry!" Rosalind could hear her voice rise in alarm.

"Yes," said Arthur. "Unfortunately Martin came upon him first, lying on the floor in Mr. Goodwin's kitchen out there in the annexe."

"He's dead?"

Arthur nodded slowly.

"But how?"

"Looks as if he's poisoned himself," said Arthur.

"Oh no." Rosalind's voice was very faint. "Then that means it must have been Garry who—" she began.

"Sorry to disillusion you," said Bernard in his very harshest tones, "but there is no evidence of any such thing. He left a suicide note stating that he loved my wife and couldn't live without her. He also wrote the words 'He poisoned her' in a very shaky hand. Presumably he was beginning to lose control of his muscles. The identity of the 'he' is not stated."

Rosalind said no more. She looked from Bernard, standing stiff and tense, to Martin shaking and gulping. There was a moment of silence in the room.

"When you've all quite finished," said Inspector Peters, who had been keenly watching this little scene, his narrow head moving from side to side, "we will continue with our enquiries."

$$— 19 —$$

Lesley Green drove Rosalind and Martin home, talking hard all the way about the events of the evening. When they arrived she looked as if she would like to come in and go on talking, but Rosalind thanked her and got rid of her, saying that Martin was too ill to sit up any longer and that she felt fit for nothing but bed herself. In fact she could not bear to listen to any more. Lesley's barely disguised conviction that Bernard had killed his wife was a grim portent of what the reaction of the rest of the village community was going to be. It was obviously going to have to be faced, and perhaps Bernard's arrest would have to be faced too, but for tonight Rosalind felt she deserved a respite.

Martin's sickness was not simply an excuse. He had been in a state of nervous collapse all the time Inspector Peters had been making his further enquiries, and the police doctor had suggested that Rosalind should give him a stiff whisky and get him to bed. In fact she would have preferred him to take one of her sleeping tablets but he refused to do so, and also refused to let her do anything for him at all. In the end she was obliged to leave him to himself and could only hope that exhaustion would eventually take over and that he would get some rest.

When the front doorbell rang at nine o'clock the following morning Martin was fast asleep and Rosalind came downstairs in her dressing-gown, yawning and confused.

"It's cruel to get you up after such a night," said Arthur

when she opened the door, "but it's really rather urgent so if you don't mind me coming in for a moment . . ."

"Of course. Tea? I haven't had any yet."

Arthur accepted tea. "This isn't exactly a social call," he said, "but it isn't exactly official either. Inspector Peters is officially in charge of the enquiries, but he's asked me to find out what I can, knowing the village and the people so much better than he does. So I have to warn you that I'm on the side of finding out the truth—as if you needed telling that!—but you know that within these limits if there's any way I can help you and your lad I'll do my very best."

"Thanks, Arthur," said Rosalind. "It's a great relief to know that you're dealing with it."

"Not dealing with it," he corrected. "Just sniffing round and trying to prevent it causing any damage to our village life here. You can't stop people talking, of course, but I'll do my best to see it doesn't go beyond certain limits. And the quicker we can clear things up the better. That's where Martin comes in. He never got round to telling the Inspector anything last night. Only about pouring out the brandy, and one or two other matters that were in everybody's statements."

"You think he knows something?" faltered Rosalind.

"It was you who gave me the idea," said the constable reproachfully.

"Yes. You're right. And if he won't tell you himself I'll have to tell you as much as I know or suspect. But first of all could you tell me something. Do they know yet how Mrs. Goodwin died?"

"Yes. It was from a combination of alcohol and a plant poison obtained from a form of water dropwort. There was more of it in the bottle of apricot brandy and in the other glasses."

Rosalind shuddered. "So if we'd all drunk our liqueurs . . ."

"It's by no means certain that it would have had the same result. You would all have been ill, certainly, possibly very ill, but it would not necessarily have been fatal. Mrs. Goodwin had already taken a large quantity of alcohol before she drank the glass of liqueur. It was the combination that killed her, with the alcohol enchancing the effect of the poison."

"All the same," said Rosalind, "it was putting everyone to a terrible risk."

"It was indeed," agreed Arthur sombrely.

"I suppose," went on Rosalind, "that whoever put it in the brandy bottle might have been determined to make sure that nobody else actually drank any. Or they might not have expected anybody but Mrs. Goodwin to drink it, which is what would have happened if Lesley Green had turned up on time. We'd all have felt obliged to have some of her elderberry wine."

"Very true. These factors are being taken into account."

"Then who does the Inspector think—" began Rosalind and hastily interrupted herself. "No, I mustn't ask that. What about Garry? How did he die?"

"From the same poison, or combination of poisons. The extract from the plant had been drunk along with gin. The empty bottle was found by his side."

"And he took it himself, intentionally?"

"That would appear to be the assumption," said Arthur cautiously, "when taken in conjunction with the note he left."

"I don't suppose he died as quickly as Jane did," said Rosalind. "He hadn't been drinking all day. We might have saved him if we'd gone to look for him at once."

"I think it's unlikely. The evidence is that he died fairly quickly. The essence of the plant was a lot more concentrated than in the apricot brandy. Apparently it is an exceptionally virulent poison—the most lethal of all our British plants, and there is no known antidote to it."

"That's what Mr. Goodwin said," muttered Rosalind.

"When did he say this?" Arthur wanted to know.

"The first time Martin and I went to Bell House. When we looked round the stillroom and Martin asked about poisonous plants. Oh my God!" Rosalind added with a quick little indrawn breath.

Arthur waited expectantly for a little while but Rosalind said no more. She wanted to tell him everything but her vocal cords seemed to have gone on strike and she was as speechless as Garry had been.

"Never mind," said Arthur in his most comfortable way.

"Don't let's worry about that for the moment. There's another matter that I'd like to ask you about and I can promise you that it won't distress you so badly. It's not very important and is probably quite irrelevant, but I'd be glad of your help all the same. It's this. Did you at any time when Mr. Goodwin was showing you round the premises see any marijuana growing anywhere?"

"Marijuana?" echoed Rosalind stupidly.

"That's right. I was talking to you about it not so long ago. Bit of an epidemic of growing it in the village."

"Oh yes. You thought Martin might have been experimenting. But he wasn't."

"No indeed. He's got too much sense for that. Did Mr. Goodwin ever mention it at all?"

"Not that I can remember," said Rosalind. "Why?"

"Well, there's no harm in telling you. I've got the Inspector's authority, but I'd be grateful if you'd keep it to yourself for the time being. You see, when some of our chaps were searching the premises and taking photographs and so on, they came upon these pots set into the ground in that little herb garden near the summer-house, and I just wondered if you'd noticed them, or any other specimens of the same plant, growing in the grounds or outhouses at Bell House when you were there before."

"I don't think I did," said Rosalind, "but I wouldn't like to swear to it because I don't know whether I'd recognize the plant."

Arthur produced some photographs. "Anything like these?"

Rosalind studied them carefully and then shook her head. "No, I don't think so," she said. "I'm almost sure I saw no plants like these. Certainly not in the spot where you mention."

"Thank you," said Arthur putting the pictures away.

"What does Mr. Goodwin say about it?" A sudden thought had struck Rosalind: a very illuminating and very disturbing thought.

"Mr. Goodwin denies all knowledge of the marijuana plants. He swears he has never grown any in his life and is not the least interested in doing so."

"I'm sure that's true."

"Between ourselves, Mrs. Bannister, so am I; nevertheless the plants were there. Planted, you might say." And the police constable gave a mild chuckle, in which Rosalind joined.

"If somebody did 'plant' them with a view to discrediting Mr. Goodwin," he continued, "I suppose you've no idea who it might be?"

Rosalind had only too clear an idea. The light of revelation was beginning to burn ever more brightly.

"Look," she said appealingly, "I'd like to tell you exactly what's in my mind, but I know you will have to tell the Inspector. Of course he'll have to know in the end, and I'm certainly not trying to conceal anything, but I feel that I should like to talk to a solicitor before I actually tell you or Inspector Peters. Would that be in order?"

"Perfectly in order. Have you anyone in mind? Or would you like me to recommend somebody?"

"Actually I have got someone in mind," said Rosalind. "I'll fix it up straight away and get in touch with you as soon as I've seen him. Is that all right?"

Arthur stood up. "I think you're taking a very wise course, Mrs. Bannister."

After he had gone Rosalind dialled Deirdre's number and the girl herself answered the phone.

"How's Martin?" she asked at once.

"Rather exhausted," replied Rosalind, wondering what version, if any, Deirdre had heard of the previous evening's events, "but basically all right."

"They don't suspect that—" began Deirdre and then stopped.

"I don't think we'd better talk on the phone," said Rosalind. "Why I rang was to ask if there was any chance of seeing your father today. This morning if possible."

"He's in the office. I'll give you the number. But, Rosalind—" Deirdre stopped again.

"Yes, my dear?"

"Are you quite sure Martin's all right? Is there anything I can do?"

Rosalind thought quickly. "Yes," she said. "If your father can see me now, I'll have to go into Brighton and leave Martin alone, and I'd rather not do that. Would you come and stay with him?"

"I'm coming at once," said Deirdre and rang off.

Rosalind had only just finished washing and dressing when she arrived, bursting with questions and with anxiety for Martin.

"There's no point in pretending it isn't serious," said Rosalind, "but truly I must talk to your father before I say anything more, and I'm hoping to persuade Martin to talk to him too. He's still asleep or pretending to be."

"What shall I do when he wakes?" asked Deirdre. "I mean, how shall I behave to him?"

Rosalind replied with a question. "Do you love Martin? Really love him, I mean?"

"Oh Rosalind, how can you ask!" cried the girl reproachfully.

Rosalind put her arms round her and kissed her. "Then you needn't worry about how to behave," she said. "You'll take your cue from him and you'll do the right thing. Goodbye and good luck. I've got to run to catch that bus."

Theodore Parker had the same dark smiling eyes as his daughter and the same air of rocklikeness. His office was cool and quiet and he moved from his desk to sit in a low chair beside Rosalind. When she had finished he said: "Now let me summarize it and then we will decide together what statement you will make to the police. Your only tangible evidence against your son consists of these stained pieces of paper." He touched the envelope that Rosalind had handed him.

"And the plants that Deirdre took with her," said Rosalind.

"Yes. She's told me about that. In fact she's told me much of what you've just been saying. Let's pass now from the supposition that Martin obtained a very small amount of a poisonous liquid and go on to what happened last night at Bell House. Your theory is that Martin and Mrs. Goodwin had worked out a little plot to cause distress and embarrassment to Mr. Goodwin. It was this. A social evening was to be arranged in which a member of the police force was to be included as a guest. During the evening Mr. Goodwin would be asked to show his guests round the premises, including the garden and outhouses, and marijuana plants were to be discovered in a prominent position. Much would be made of the discovery and the policeman would be obliged to take some action. Another guest, prominent in village society, could no doubt be relied on to make the most of the situation. Mr. Goodwin, who has built up a considerable reputation for himself in his field, could be quite seriously affected by the outcome of this little plot. Is this what you think your son was up to?"

"Yes," said Rosalind, "I'm sure of it. His whole behavior, and the way he and Mrs. Goodwin looked at each other showed it. Yes. I'm absolutely sure."

"How do you think he got hold of the plants?"

"I've no idea. But he has friends of whom I know nothing. Or they might have drawn Garry into the plot, although I think this is unlikely because Mrs. Goodwin was playing off the two boys against each other and Garry was desperately jealous of Martin, whom he saw as usurping his own place with her. I'm quite sure of that too."

"Right. We now come to Mrs. Goodwin's death. The marijuana plot hardly fits in with putting hemlock extract into apricot brandy. That looks like the work of another hand than your son's."

"That's what I thought," said Rosalind, "but I wish I could be sure."

"I suppose," said Mr. Parker, "that it is possible the poison in the brandy was the same as that extracted by Martin from the plants stolen from the house, but I am not in the confidence of the police and I have no idea whether they have yet traced the source of the poison. Speaking in ignorance, both of the police enquiries and of the exact nature of the poison, I would have thought that whatever Martin managed to extract would be too little to have any effect if poured into a full bottle of liqueur, although of course it might have been lethal if taken neat. I would have said that there must have been more poisonous extract added to that brandy than Martin's little bit. I don't know if this will be of any comfort to you."

"I don't know either," said Rosalind. She thought for a moment and then went on. "Mr. Parker, I'm going to tell you something else, although I expect you'll have guessed it. I have not come entirely on Martin's account. I'm here on Mr. Goodwin's as well, although he doesn't know it and presumably he has his own solicitor if necessary. I've told you about Martin's feelings towards Mr. Goodwin and what I think they led to, but I haven't told you about Martin's behaviour after Jane Goodwin's death. He instantly accused Mr. Goodwin of causing it. Whether this was just shock or whether it was a deliberate attempt to harm Mr. Goodwin, or whether he really believed it, I don't know, but he is persisting in these accusations."

"Are they backed up by anything? Has he any positive evidence?"

"I'm quite sure he hasn't," said Rosalind. "If he had, he would have told the police at once. There's only one possibility I can think of."

"Yes?" said Mr. Parker encouragingly.

"It's a most terrible thing to say about my own son," said Rosalind unhappily, "but there's no sense in seeking your help if I'm going to hold anything back. I can't help wondering whether Martin has done anything to fake evidence against Mr. Goodwin. I can't think what, or how, or when, but I'm afraid it's not impossible."

"You can't be more specific?"

Rosalind shook her head. "I wish I could."

"Was there, for example, any time after Mrs. Goodwin's death when Martin was not in the room with the rest of you?"

"Yes, when he went off on his own to look for Garry. Mr. Goodwin and the Inspector were upstairs and the other policemen hadn't yet arrived, and our village constable went after Martin, but not for several minutes. It was actually Martin who found Garry dead in the shed. We none of us knew where he was going and he might have had as much as five minutes completely to himself before anybody else found both him and Garry. Ever since then he's been in this dreadful state. Of course it was a great shock finding Garry dead on top of Jane's death, and I suppose it could account for Martin being so sick, but it might be something more than shock that is making him like this. It might be conscience too. I know my son, Mr. Parker," said Rosalind, leaning forward and speaking very earnestly, "and I know the form his fits of conscience have taken in the past when he's done something he's ashamed of but hasn't wanted to admit it. It's always been this sort of sickness. On the other hand he's pretty good at coping with shock. When my husband died it was an unbelievable shock to both of us. You'll know about it, no doubt. Martin was only fifteen but he took it wonderfully after the first reaction. He doesn't go to pieces when horrible things happen. But he does go to pieces if he feels guilty. I know that's not evidence to you, but to me it's a pretty strong proof."

"I respect your opinion," said Deirdre's father, "and I admire your courage in telling me this. So you think that anything Martin might have done after Mrs. Goodwin's death was in some way connected with the mute boy, Garry?"

"It looks like it," said Rosalind. "I suppose he could have planted the marijuana when he ran off as if to look for Garry, but that would have taken time, and in any case they would surely have seen to it earlier. I would think Jane Goodwin attended to it. It would be easier for her to choose the right moment, being on the premises. No, I think Martin must have done something in the stillroom, where Garry was found dead, but it need not necessarily have been anything to do with Garry. Martin might have been putting a bottle of poisonous liquid with Mr. Goodwin's fingerprints on it in some prominent position. Something like that."

"The police are very good at seeing through faked evidence," said Mr. Parker. "Don't underestimate them. And by your own account Martin is not particularly thorough or careful, even when he has plenty of time. If you are right about this, it will soon come to light, though of course it would be much better if he could be persuaded to admit it himself. In that case it might be possible to arrange that no charge is made against him."

"How serious could the charge be?" asked Rosalind.

"It depends," said Mr. Parker, "very much on how serious a view the police take of it, and of course on the attitude of the person most injured or liable to be injured by any action Martin may have taken."

"I'm sure Mr. Goodwin would not want to charge him," said Rosalind. "Oh, if only we could get him to talk!"

"Perhaps Deirdre has already succeeded. Now I'm going to make a suggestion. I'm going to drive you straight back to Swallowfields now and if Deirdre hasn't yet made any headway with Martin, then I'm going to frighten him into coming clean. This has got to be dealt with at once, before the Inspector gets on him again and he puts his foot even more deeply into it. No, don't protest, Mrs. Bannister. My partners can take over all my business here. This is much more important. I've a personal interest too, you know. My daughter's happiness is very much bound up with your son."

"I know," said Rosalind, "and I know he cares for her very much. This other business was only a sort of temporary madness. And I was largely responsible for it."

She didn't explain why, and Mr. Parker didn't ask. Deirdre will have told him about Bernard and me, thought Rosalind, and he'll have gathered the rest from the story I've just been telling him. I wonder if he believes me. I wonder if he suspects me of killing Jane myself. After all, I've got just as much motive as Bernard. But nobody would expect Martin to fake evidence against his own mother. Or would they? After all, I very nearly faked some against him in order to try to get him to confess.

While Mr. Parker manoeuvred the car quickly through the heaviest traffic and turned off along the road to Swallowfields, Rosalind's thoughts went round and round. In the centre of them was a strong conviction that whatever came of it she had done the right thing in telling Mr. Parker everything. But her doubts and her guilt and her apprehension and her irreconcilable love for Martin and for Bernard all beat and beat against this firm rock of certainty, trying their hardest to knock it off balance or to wear it away.

20

Deirdre clung to her father and cried, "Thank God you've come! Martin's disappeared!"

"How and when?" asked Mr. Parker.

"About twenty minutes ago. He got dressed and had some coffee but wouldn't eat anything and we were sitting talking in the kitchen. I didn't ask him any questions, just waited for him to ask me. He wanted to know where you'd gone, Rosalind, and I thought it best to tell the truth, but I didn't give any details. I just said, to ask Dad's advice about Mrs. Goodwin's death before the police came round again asking questions. I hoped he'd ask me what I thought, which would have given me a lead in, but he didn't, so I just waited. Then he suddenly said, Hadn't they arrested Bernard Goodwin yet? And I said, Not that I knew of. Then he got very angry and said they ought to have arrested him, and what did my father think. So I had to be very careful and I answered that the police didn't make an arrest without some pretty good evidence, and Martin cried, "But they've got evidence! Look at Garry's note!" I said I didn't know anything about Garry's note, and he said that it said plainly enough that Bernard Goodwin had killed his wife."

At this point, Deirdre, who had been talking very quickly and excitedly, paused for breath, and her father said: "I hope you pointed out that a written accusation is no stronger

173

evidence than a spoken accusation, and that there is such a thing as a law of slander?"

"I did say that, Dad. And I said something like heaven help us if we're going to be arrested for murder just because somebody says or writes that we did it. You see, I was getting a bit angry with him by now—angry as well as worried. And he was beginning to get angry with me too for refusing to say that Bernard Goodwin had killed his wife, and then he suddenly started shivering and I asked if he was all right and he said he felt chilly and feverish again and would I go upstairs and get him a sweater. Oh Dad! I should have guessed. But I didn't. When I got back he'd gone. The front door was open and the gate was open but there was no sign of him either in the main road or up the lane. He must have run like mad, and first I thought of starting the car and driving about looking for him and then I thought that was no good because he might have gone on a footpath or got a bus or anything, and you'd be worried stiff if you got here and found no one. So I rang the office, and they said you'd just left and I thought I'd better wait till you got here."

"You did quite right, my love," said Mr. Parker.

"I'm so glad," said Deirdre. "I did wonder if I ought to tell the police straight away."

"We will probably have to do so eventually, but let's give it a little longer first. What do you suggest, Mrs. Bannister? Have you any idea at all where Martin might have gone?"

"There's only one place I can think of, and that's Bell House," said Rosalind. "Either to plant some more evidence or to tackle Bernard direct."

Deirdre gave a little gasp. "Oh no!"

"Right," said Deirdre's father. "We'll go there straight away."

In the big sitting-room at Bell House Bernard and Martin stood facing each other. The older man looked pale and exhausted, his face lined and strained, and his eyes had lost all sparkle. The boy looked ill too, but there was about him an air of feverish restlessness, and he dug his fingers into the pockets of his jeans as if he needed to keep them under control.

"They're going to arrest you," he said. "It's only a matter of time. I've just heard that from our solicitors."

Bernard made no reply.

"Don't you care that they're going to arrest you?" cried Martin, his voice rising hysterically.

"If you want to talk to the Inspector, he's only just left here, but no doubt he'll be delighted to make an early appointment with you." Bernard's voice sounded very weary but there was a sarcastic note in it that goaded the boy to further uncontrol.

"I don't want to see the police!" he shouted. "I'm trying to tell you they're going to charge you with murdering Jane!"

"You are in their confidence? That's more than I am."

Martin's hands came out of his pockets and looked as if they would like to make their way to Bernard's throat. The older man stood looking at the boy's movement with contemptuous eyes. Martin dropped his arms and began to move jerkily about the room.

"I could get you off," he said in a voice slightly more under control.

"Really?"

"I know something that will get you off but I'm not going to tell them unless you promise—" He broke off and waited, but Bernard said nothing.

"If you promise to leave my mother alone, I'll tell the police something that will get you off," said Martin hurriedly.

When Bernard spoke at last his voice was icy. "If you have any information that can throw any light on the death of my wife, it is your duty to inform the police immediately."

"Don't you want to be saved from arrest?" Martin was beginning to sound desperate and his hands were moving again.

"I repeat, it is your duty to tell the police everything you know."

"You bastard!" shouted Martin, rushing at Bernard with both arms flailing. "You bloody well leave my mother alone! She was perfectly happy—we were all perfectly happy till you came along."

He hit out so wildly that Bernard was able to sidestep without any difficulty. The next blow was more effective and

caught Bernard on the shoulder. He made an effort to catch
Martin by the arms and cried: "Stop it! Stop it, you idiot! This
settles nothing. Sit down and we'll talk."

But Martin was past talking. He began to hit wildly but with
great force, many of the blows missing their mark, but others
of them doing damage, and the older man had no recourse left
but to defend himself as best he could.

Theodore Parker's powerful car quickly covered the distance
from the centre of Swallowfields to Bell House. Rosalind and
Deirdre sat together in the back, gripping hands. None of them
spoke except when Rosalind pointed out which road to take.

The big house looked as solid and comfortable as it had the
first time Rosalind had seen it. There were no cars in the drive
and the whole place seemed very quiet after all the activity of
the previous night. Theodore Parker rang the bell and then rang
again, more loudly, after waiting in vain for a reply. He was
just about to suggest to Rosalind that they should go round the
garden and up to the annexe when there was a loud cry from
Deirdre, who had moved away from the front doorstep towards
the nearer of the bay windows of the sitting-room. They were
old-fashioned sash windows, only a few feet from the ground.
The central sash was pushed up a little way, and as Rosalind
and Mr. Parker ran towards Deirdre they saw her push it up
further and swing herself on to the window-ledge and climb
into the room.

"Martin! Stop it!" they heard her scream as they reached the
open window and saw what she had seen.

Bernard was sprawled over the settee, lying limply with his
hand trailing to the floor. Martin was bending over him with
his hands round Bernard's throat. In the same moment that
Deirdre flung herself upon Martin, Mr. Parker called out in a
loud and authoritative voice: "Open up! It's the police here!"

Martin loosened his grip, turned around, and stared at
Deirdre with eyes that did not recognize her. She took a step
forward and flung her arms around him and cried: "It's all
right, Martin. Everything's going to be all right."

Suddenly he began to tremble violently and the two watching at the window could see from his face above Deirdre's head

that he had come back to himself. Deirdre led him to an armchair and then called out that she was going to open the front door.

"I don't think he's seriously injured," said Mr. Parker a minute later, straightening up after leaning over Bernard. "We'd better get a doctor, though. Those bruises need attending to."

Bernard was in fact trying to move. Rosalind eased him into a more comfortable position while Mr. Parker telephoned. He opened one eye—the other was blackened and swollen—and Rosalind could see that he had recognized her. His mouth moved as if he were about to speak, but no sound came. She smiled at him and laid her finger on his lips. "Keep quiet. Keep still. The doctor won't be long."

When Bernard had been attended to and told to rest the doctor stood looking down at Martin. "He needs sedating too," he said to Rosalind. "I'll give him something that'll send him off for a while."

For the first time since he had been interrupted in his murderous onslaught on Bernard, Martin spoke.

"I don't want any dope," he said, shakily but clearly. "I want to be fully conscious. There's something I've got to tell Deirdre."

"All right," said the doctor. "I'll leave you to it." He dug in his case and produced a sachet of capsules and handed them to Rosalind. "Give him these if he changes his mind. One every four hours."

"I'll see you out," said Theodore Parker.

He was gone for some time, talking to the doctor in the drive, and extracting a promise to keep quiet about what had just been happening during the last hour at Bell House. Meanwhile Martin said to his mother, "D'you mind going away for a bit? I only want to talk to Deirdre."

Rosalind got up to leave the room. At the door she glanced back and saw that Deirdre had sat down on the arm of Martin's chair. She had one arm round his shoulders and with the other hand she was firmly holding his trembling fingers. On the girl's face as she looked down at Martin was an expression of such tenderness and strength that Rosalind found herself muttering a little prayer of gratitude. In the hall she hesitated for only a moment before going upstairs to sit by Bernard's bedside.

"Don't try to talk," she said. "It's going to be all right. Everything is sorting itself out. For us at any rate. But I can't get poor Garry out of my mind."

"I know—how—he felt," Bernard managed to croak.

"I too. When your throat's less sore, you'll have to tell me more about him, and whether there are any relatives, and whether there is anything we can do for people in his position, and so on."

Bernard nodded and then grimaced with pain.

"Not now," said Rosalind. "Keep still. There's no hurry. I'm going to stay here and look after you."

Some time later, when Bernard had drifted into sleep, Theodore Parker came in and beckoned Rosalind out of the room. "We'll go in the garden," he said, "and leave the children to comfort each other. He told Deirdre everything and then repeated the essence of it to me. I think I'll be able to sort it out without anything very drastic happening to him, and he couldn't be in better hands than Deirdre's."

"He couldn't indeed," agreed Rosalind, finding her eyes suddenly filled with tears.

"She'll keep him on the strait and narrow," said Deirdre's father as they approached the summer-house. "Let's sit in here while I tell you. Although really I think you know it all already. You were right in every detail. It's the sort of thing that happens sometimes when there's a very close bond between two people, as there was between you and Martin. He took those plant specimens, discarded the harmless ones, and extracted the liquid from the two most poisonous—the hemlock and the hemlock water dropwort—and kept it all mixed together in a tiny plastic bottle. He says Jane Goodwin had strongly hinted that he should do something like this so that they could arrange a fake poisoning attempt in which her husband could be accused. He gave her the bottle. He doesn't know what she did with it and she never mentioned it again, but she suggested the marijuana scheme instead. Someone at his school got hold of the plants for him. He didn't want to say who, and I didn't press him. Jane Goodwin did the actual planting, just before the dinner-party, managing to avoid both her husband and Garry. Now as to the mute boy—"

"Yes," broke in Rosalind. "This is what I find hardest of all to stomach."

"It's not very nice, but truly I believe that Jane Goodwin was the evil genius throughout and Martin very much a dupe. Yes, they were both of them amusing themselves at the expense of that poor boy, taunting him with his passion for the woman, rousing his jealousy to the point of desperation. Curiously enough, it never seems to have occurred to Jane Goodwin that the boy's fury could be directed against herself. All the time she was tormenting him she continued to trust him to buy her drink for her at various local pubs. He actually bought the apricot brandy at the Black Lion, where he occasionally had a game of darts with some boys he knew slightly. The bottle has a screw top and no seal. Presumably this is why he chose it. It would still look untouched after he had poured in the poisonous liquid that he had extracted in the stillroom. That would be no difficulty for him. He knew a great deal about plants and had the full run of the place for many hours completely undisturbed.

"There is no evidence at all that Garry was trying to incriminate anybody else, and why he chose that particular moment for killing the one human being he loved we shall never know. Perhaps she teased him unbearably at the dinner-party and sent him right over the edge. Neither do we know whether he was concerned that nobody else should drink the poison. I am inclined to think that he was quite sure that only Jane would drink the liqueur, and that everyone else would have elderberry wine, if anything at all. Mr. Goodwin seems to have drunk very little, and Garry could see that you don't drink much. But Martin, as you thought, had lately been absorbing a great deal of alcohol under Mrs. Goodwin's tuition. I am sorry to sound rather unforgiving, but I really do think she did a great deal of harm."

"I think she was very unhappy," said Rosalind.

"Lots of people are unhappy, but that's no reason to make other people suffer too. To return to Garry, Martin thinks it's possible he might have intended the poisoned liqueur for

Martin too, knowing that he would be the most likely to follow
Jane's lead and have some of the brandy. But when he saw it
in your hand and in Mr. Goodwin's and Arthur's, Garry must
have got a dreadful shock. Hence the horrifying attempt to
speak. At any rate, it saved you others from unpleasant
consequences. Martin thinks he was overcome by remorse as
soon as he realized that Jane was dead, and that was why he
rushed off and swallowed all the rest of the poisonous liquid
himself."

"What about the suicide note?" asked Rosalind.

"You were right again," said Mr. Parker, "although you
couldn't possibly have guessed the exact details. Martin found
Garry dead—or at any rate deeply unconscious and near
death—and beside him on the floor was a bottle, this note, and
a felt-tipped pen. The note read as follows: 'I killed her but I
loved her and I can't live without her.' That was all. Martin
said the idea came to him in a flash. He didn't touch the paper,
but held it firm on the floor by pressing the pen on it, and tore
off the top which carried the words 'I killed her but.' That left
the words 'I loved her and I can't live without her.' Martin says
he then pressed the torn off piece of paper over the remaining
piece in order to hold it steady and wrote in a fair imitation of
Garry's hand the words 'he poisoned her.' Apparently even at
that moment he couldn't quite bring himself to write Bernard
Goodwin's name, but the implication would obviously be
drawn that Mr. Goodwin had killed his wife. After that he
pocketed the scrap of paper and the pen, flicked another such
pen from the table on to the floor near where Garry lay, and
was at the door of the stillroom yelling for help by the time
your village policeman arrived. He's a bit confused about what
happened next. He knows he was violently sick and continued
to feel like death for many hours. The guilt and the self-disgust
were overwhelming. You were right about that too.

"He says he expected to be searched and was surprised that
the police didn't find the pen and the piece of paper on him. He
has given them to me, incidentally. After a very anguished
night he still felt terribly guilty this morning, but he still
couldn't overcome his hatred of Mr. Goodwin and he was also
beginning to be really afraid for himself as the realization of

what he had done came right home to him. For his own safety, his own peace of mind, it was essential that the police should believe his faked evidence. If Bernard Goodwin were arrested, this would mean that the police believed it, and Martin would be safe. How he expected to live with his conscience, he says he simply doesn't know. Your coming to talk to me got him badly rattled because he felt sure you had guessed everything, as indeed you had. Then Deirdre saying the police saw through faked evidence made him feel worse than ever. He says he rushed off to Mr. Goodwin in a state of panic, half thinking of trying to find out whether Mr. Goodwin suspected him, half thinking of confessing what he had done, but on the way the idea of trying to strike a bargain came to him, and then Mr. Goodwin's manner infuriated him and he completely lost his head."

"Bernard can be very infuriating," said Rosalind. "I believe most of it is a form of defence, but of course most people wouldn't see it that way. Truly, though, I think he was probably just terribly tired and worried to death, and was not really meaning to be particularly offensive to Martin."

"You have constituted yourself Bernard Goodwin's defending counsel," said Mr. Parker with a smile, "and I have no wish to argue with you. Fortunately no great harm was done."

"Thanks to Deirdre."

"Thanks to Deirdre. I think we've left them alone for long enough. Shall we go back?"

As they strolled back across the lawn to the back door of Bell House, Mr. Parker said, "Will you allow me to wish you some happiness in your future life, Mrs. Bannister?"

"Happiness? With two people dead?"

"I think you will be too wise to let that worry you for ever," said Mr. Parker.

"Is it wisdom, or is it selfishness?"

"My dear Mrs. Bannister, I should love to have a philosophical discussion with you some time when we are less preoccupied. If our children are going to join their lives together, it looks as if we shall have every chance of getting to know each other better. I know my wife will be more than delighted, and

I am going to claim your company and Martin's to a family meal exactly one week from today."

Rosalind thanked him.

"Pamela and I will greatly look forward to it," he went on, "and I know she will provide us with an exciting meal. Martin will bear witness to that. I can also promise you one thing more."

He paused, and Rosalind looked at him enquiringly.

"Extract of hemlock will not be on the menu," said Mr. Parker as he pushed open the door.